pleasure control

Also by Cathryn Fox

PLEASURE EXCHANGE
PLEASURE PROLONGED

pleasure control

cathryn *fox*

red
AVON
An Imprint of HarperCollinsPublishers

PLEASURE CONTROL. Copyright © 2006 by Cathryn Fox. Excerpt from *Pleasure Prolonged* copyright © 2007 by Cathryn Fox. All rights reserved. Printed in the United States of America. No part of this book may be used or reproduced in any manner whatsoever without written permission except in the case of brief quotations embodied in critical articles and reviews. For information address HarperCollins Publishers, 10 East 53rd Street, New York, NY 10022.

HarperCollins books may be purchased for educational, business, or sales promotional use. For information please write: Special Markets Department, HarperCollins Publishers, 10 East 53rd Street, New York, NY 10022.

FIRST AVON RED EDITION PUBLISHED 2006, REISSUED 2013.

Interior text designed by Diahann Sturge

The Library of Congress has cataloged the original paperback edition as follows:

Fox, Cathryn.
    Pleasure control / by Cathryn Fox.—1st ed.
        p. cm.
ISBN-13: 978-0-06-089856-4
ISBN-10: 0-06-089856-9
I. Title

PR9199.4.F69P55 2006
823'.92—dc22   2006007495

ISBN 978-0-06-226558-6

13 14 15 16 17   WBC/RRD   10 9 8 7 6 5 4 3 2 1

Alex, for your wicked sense of humor
and making me laugh every single day.

Allison, for filling my life
with rainbows and butterflies.

I love you both!

Acknowledgments

There are so many people who have supported me in my journey to publication. The following is just the beginning of a very long list:

Lori Foster for her novella contest. Thank you for all your guidance and support and for loving my story in your contest. You are an inspiration to all.

My fabulous agent, **Bob Diforio**. Thank you for all you do and for always keeping me in the loop.

My wonderful editor, **Lucia Macro**. Thank you for loving my stories and for being such a pleasure to work with.

Acknowledgments

My husband, **Mark**, who always believed in me. I love you.

Shelly Hutchinson. Thank you for your friendship, your support, your genius, and the word "had."

Paula Altenburg. Thank you for being there for me, for reading every draft, and for your impeccable grammar.

Heather Veinotte. Thank you for buying and reading all those erotic romances so you'd better understand my stories. The things you have to do for friends!

Julianne MacLean. Thank you for that wonderful day at the pool where you helped me brainstorm ideas.

Lisa Renee Jones. Thank you for your guidance, support, and friendship. You're a gem.

ML Benton. Thank you for your friendship and creative genius with my website, blog, and newsletter.

Susie Murphy. For being a friend as well as a wonderful, supportive sister. I love you.

Allure Authors. Thank you for all your support. You ladies rock!

RWAC Goals group. Thank you all for keeping me on track!

Chapter 1

How could so many women be looking to curb their husbands' sexual appetite?

Laura Manning pondered that question as she flicked off her Bunsen burner and curled her fingers around the warm glass test tube that held her future. She swirled vial number twenty-four in her palms and arched an eyebrow at her lab partner, Jay Cutler.

"Sure you don't want *me* to do this?"

Jay raked his fingers through his midnight hair. His sensuous mouth curved downward. "The libido suppressant we're cooking up is for guys, Laura." His eyes swept over her curves as he shifted his stance. "Trust me, you don't qualify by a long shot. And anyway, the Grant

Governing Board will tank your career, and mine, if we don't show them something concrete by the end of next week."

Laura gnawed on her bottom lip, the way she always did when she was frustrated. Of course, he was right. They hadn't spent the last few months working long into the night for the board to suddenly red-light the project.

She sat on a stool and planted her elbows on the stainless steel work counter. "But we don't know all the side effects yet."

Jay reached out and closed his hand over hers. The sharp angles of his face softened when their eyes met. "And we'll never know unless I play guinea pig."

He squeezed her fingers and brushed his thumb over her skin. The touch was innocent, really, but it didn't stop the shock waves from pulsing through her. Shivers of warm need tingled all the way down to her toes. The already too small lab seemed to close in on her.

Even though his touch played some mysterious alchemy with her libido, she knew he didn't go for nerdy science girls like her. For the last three years she'd watched enough women fawning all over him to know Mr. Different-Woman-Every-Week had a ravenous appetite for tall, waify blondes with big toothy smiles that were, ultimately, the brightest thing about them. Her intelligence and petite, curvaceous frame were the antithesis of what he gravitated toward.

Honestly, couldn't men figure out that all good things came in bright, small packages? Her glance drifted downward and halted just below Jay's belt. Well, maybe not *all* things.

The heat from his thumb idly stroking her skin pulled her thoughts back. She jumped up and reached for a syringe. "Okay, if you're game, then let's get this over with. Grab a seat and roll up your sleeve." Motioning for him to take the stool beside hers, she prepared the serum.

She drew the potion into the needle, removed the air bubbles, and met his gaze straight on. "All set?"

"Prick me, Laura."

She ripped open an alcohol swab and swiped his bicep. Oh my! And what a lovely bicep it was.

"But be gentle. I've seen the way you give needles." The sexy cock of his head scattered her thoughts. "We're just lucky there haven't been any casualties yet." Humor edged his voice and played down her spine like a powerful aphrodisiac.

Ignoring the tingle flowing through her bloodstream, she bit back a grin, tossed him an annoyed look, and held up the syringe. "There's always a first."

He leaned into her and opened his mouth to speak, but

she wagged her index finger and cut him off before he could come back with some smart-assed comment.

She arched a warning brow. "Play nice or I'll trade this in for a dull one."

When would their easy banter and friendly jibes finally stop stirring her insides? Working closely with him for the last three years had not always been an easy task. At times she was certain root canal would have been less torturous. Whenever he gifted her with one of his casual, sexy grins, her body would ache to join with his, making it difficult to summon a modicum of concentration. Fortunately, they rarely spent any time together outside the lab. Such prolonged exposure to "Wildman" Jay Cutler would scorch her body more than a week in the blazing summer sun without SPF. Honestly, the man should come with a warning label.

They were, however, required to make an appearance at a monthly bonding session that Director Reginald Smith insisted all employees attend. Like Reginald always preached, "By bonding outside the workplace, we accept happiness and harmony into our lives." Good Lord! Step aside, Dr. Phil.

After she filled his muscle with the syrupy concoction, she covered the pinprick with a Band-Aid and sat back on her stool. "Now we wait." She turned her attention to her notebook and began jotting down the data.

He pitched his voice low. "Wait for what?"

She lifted her chin to look at him. "To *see*"—she stretched that last word out and nodded toward his crotch—"if Little Jay gets aroused."

"*Little Jay?*" A rakish smile touched his lips. "More like *not-so-little-Jay*, and don't you think we should put him to the test?"

Laura twisted sideways and glanced over her shoulder. "There must be a magazine around here somewhere to help you with that *small* problem," she teased.

He folded his arms in defiance, his lips curled. "I don't think so."

"Perhaps you should call one of your many girlfriends." What had been meant to sound professional came out sounding rather sarcastic, jealous. Damn.

Jay sidled closer. Close enough to overwhelm her senses with his hypnotic scent. He looked deep into her eyes and gazed at her with such intensity that ripples of sensual pleasure danced over her flesh.

"Did you forget this project is top secret, Laura? If *Little Jay*, as you so kindly named him, goes AWOL while I'm having sex, don't you think my date would get just a little suspicious?"

Okay, so apparently he'd never suffered from a bout of impotence. That didn't really surprise her. Thrill her? Yes. Surprise her? No. Too bad the last guy she'd dated couldn't claim the same victory. That whole relationship had played out like a romantic comedy, without the romance. She'd only been serious with two guys and neither one of them had ever taken the time to satisfy her sexually. The kind of men she attracted only cared about their own pleasures and left her needing to take matters into her own hands. *Literally*. Now she simply avoided the dating scene. Why bother with the middleman when she could go straight to ecstasy with her battery-operated best friend?

Jay's leg shifted and brushed against hers. A fine tremor moved through her as she reacted to his touch. Mercy!

Perhaps she'd pick up extra batteries on the way home.

Laura had never had casual sex in her life, but if Jay was offering his services, that would certainly make her rethink things. Because judging by the number of women who'd called the lab after a night with him, she knew he wasn't the kind of guy who'd leave a woman high and dry.

Slick, wet, and satisfied, yes. High and dry, never.

She shrugged and focused her thoughts. "You're a resourceful guy. If you deflate, just make up an excuse."

His head descended; his lips, warm and silky, hovered only inches from hers. She found his total disregard for her personal space titillating and began to quiver in her most private places.

"I have a better idea," he said.

The heat in his eyes intrigued her. "Really?" Did that

idea involve the two of them naked and a bottle of chocolate syrup? Lord knows she was always open to ideas involving chocolate, or syrup, or the two of them naked.

"Yeah, a really great idea." Exquisite pleasure swept over her when his hair brushed against the nape of her neck. Eyes fixated on hers, he fingered her pristine white lab coat. "I think you should take this off, go home, and have a long, hot bubble bath."

In a motion so fast it caught her off guard, he pulled the plastic clip from her tightly coiled bun, allowing her long chestnut curls to tumble over her shoulders.

Without pause, he continued. "Then I want you to slip into your silkiest lingerie."

He was kidding, right? He'd never given her a second glance before. She wasn't even his type.

"Well . . . ?" he asked. "Are you game?"

What made him think she'd be willing to turn into slut-in-silk for their research? For him?

Okay, so she'd be willing. But there was no freaking way she was going to admit to him just how willing she was.

She shook her head to clear it. Surely she was suffering from delusions, probably a side effect from working with the suppressant.

He *had* to be kidding.

The devil's grin spread across his handsome face. "If I don't get aroused, we'll know the potion worked."

So he wasn't kidding.

Trying for casual, she tipped her chin to look him square in the eyes. "And if you do get aroused?"

A playful glint danced in his eyes as his gaze roamed over her. When he reached out to caress her cheek with his thumb, a torrid heat seeped into her skin. Laura moistened her lips and tried to ignore the elevated thud of her pulse.

His bad-boy gaze settled on her mouth. "Sweetheart, if I do get aroused, the possibilities are endless."

Chapter 2

Jay tucked a bottle of red wine under his arm and climbed the stairs to Laura's apartment two at a time. He'd thought of nothing else all day except what her curvaceous body would look like dressed in silky lingerie. He felt his semi-erect cock grow another inch just imagining it now. His flesh lubricated in anticipation as each footstep took him closer to her door.

Seeing her half naked for research purposes was pure bullshit and he knew it. Although he had to admit doing it in the name of science certainly put an erotic spin on things.

There was something about Laura Manning that physically pulled at him the way no other woman had. She was a lethal combination of intelligence, innocence, and sensuality.

She got under his skin and warmed his body like a quick shot of brandy. He had it bad for her. So bad, in fact, that for the past couple of months he hadn't even had the inclination to go on another date. The calluses on his palms were proof of that. Casual sex had lost its appeal when all he could think about was how he wanted to be palming the contours of a woman who was soft and curvy, sweet and sexy.

Even though he felt an overwhelming physical attraction to Laura, it wasn't like he would ever develop a deeper emotional bond with her. Like his father and the rest of the Cutler men before him, he wasn't cut out for lifelong commitment. Lord knows his mother had beaten that fact into him. Not one of the Cutler men in his father's generation had ever had a lasting relationship. After his father bailed on the family, his mother referred to the clan as the "Cold-Hearted Cutlers."

Jay knew his mother despised him, likely because he was the spitting image of his father. She repeatedly assured him he'd grow up to follow in the Cutler footsteps. The only people who had faith in him and believed he would grow into a fine, respectable man were his childhood best friend Dino Moretti and Dino's parents, Tony and Isabella. He spent more time at their Italian restaurant than he did at his own house. Being around them gave him a glimpse of how others lived and loved.

Jay had always treated the women he dated with respect, but since he never felt any deep emotions for them, he assumed his mother was right—he was a chip off the old block, just another Cutler who thought with his penis and was incapable of true, emotional love.

As he approached Laura's door, his thoughts once again returned to the sexy woman awaiting his arrival. God, he craved the feel of her skin next to his. The way she moved with unintentional sensuality and the way her raspberry scent stirred his hormones nearly drove him over the edge. He was dying to find out if she tasted as sweet as she smelled.

Working long into the nights with her had proven to be an exercise in frustration. Around the laboratory she was known as the Ice Princess, a woman who only wanted to research sex inside the lab, not out. She'd never once given him any indication that she was interested in a relationship with him, physical or otherwise. He respected that and had kept his hands to himself. Until now. Until the opportunity to take this relationship to the next level of intimacy had presented itself.

Christ, if she was dressed in white lace when he walked through that door, he knew he'd have to call on every ounce of strength he had not to bend her over and take her sensuous body right there.

He tugged his T-shirt out from his waistband, letting it cover the bulge tenting his jeans. Fuck, he'd been flying at half mast for months now. If he didn't soon tame the raging anaconda between his legs, he was going to rupture an artery, not to mention all the test tubes he'd come close to knocking over at the lab. His dick was as hard as a torpedo and capable of taking out anything in its path.

His perma-boner indicated that the potion hadn't yet begun to work. Of course, it wasn't that he didn't want it to work. He did. Their future careers at Iowa Research Center depended on it. Not to mention the fact that they wanted to perfect the top secret suppressant before Ad-Tech, their rivals, got wind of their project. He just wanted it to hold off for a few hours so he could coax Laura into succumbing to her needs, her desires. Desires he suspected she had but continually denied.

Tonight he was on a mission. He planned on taking their research out of the lab and into the bedroom. He planned on turning the Ice Princess into a puddle of molten liquid.

Tingles of excitement warmed Laura's blood as she paced around her small apartment anxiously awaiting Jay's arrival. She'd almost worn a hole in her carpet as well as her new thigh-high white stockings.

She drew a breath and smoothed her hair off her face.

Her palms were so damp they moistened her curls. Laura wiped her hands over her housecoat, letting the thick terry cotton drink in her moisture.

Good Lord, what had she been thinking, agreeing to something like this? The director would kick them to the curb if he found out they were testing the serum on themselves. Especially since they had yet to achieve positive results with their lab rats, the first stage in the analysis process. Obviously her brain had ceased to function and the damp triangular patch at the juncture of her legs was now calling all the shots.

In all honesty, she was simply a quiet, law-abiding, career-oriented woman, raised in a loving middle-class family who never took risks and had never done anything so reckless.

So naughty.

So delightfully scandalous.

For the hundredth time she glanced at the clock, then walked over to her window. She pulled back the sheer curtain and scanned her surroundings. High overhead, silvery stars dotted the velvety black canvas. The full moon broke through the canopy of oak leaves fringing her walkway and lit up the empty path leading to the main entrance. Resuming her pacing, she walked to the door and looked through the peephole.

She stopped to consider what she'd gotten herself into.

In no time at all the man she was secretly infatuated with would be walking through her front door, expecting to see her in her slinkiest lingerie.

And what were the chances she'd ever experience the feel of his lips caressing hers, or his artful fingers trailing over her heated, naked flesh? None, considering the fact that she'd given him a libido suppressant hours earlier.

She resisted the urge to slap her forehead. Way to go, Laura. You're brilliant. That move had Nobel Prize written all over it.

But what if he did get aroused?

The possibilities are endless.

Those four simple words had echoed in her head all day. She allowed herself a brief luxurious moment to envision what it would be like to have his naked body moving over hers. His mouth kissing a path down her quivering flesh until he reached the moist fissure between her thighs. The soft blade of his tongue opening her dewy folds so he could taste her liquid arousal. His lips closing over her hooded flesh, branding her with their heat, claiming her as his own.

Her skin came alive as a wave of desire traveled onward and upward through her body. Laura shook her passion-fogged mind from its delicious wanderings and retraced her steps back to the window.

Actually, if she really thought about it, she was in a

win/win situation. If Jay didn't get aroused, they'd secure their funding and make their mark in the scientific world. If he did get aroused, well . . . a slow tremor made her body quake . . . maybe he could douse the fire raging between her legs.

Which one did she want more?

She reached for the curtain. Her fingers froze in midair when a soft knock on her door drew her attention. She spun around and sucked in a quick, sharp breath. Her pulse leapt in her throat.

God, she was a bundle of nerves. It wasn't every day her job required her to entice the guy she'd been fantasizing about for months. A guy who was completely out of her league.

She tightened her robe around her waist and slowly padded across the floor. Slipping her hand around the knob, she twisted it open and eyed the man casually lounging against her doorjamb.

She took a moment to peruse the length of him. Sculpted muscles stretched the cotton fabric of his T-shirt while broad shoulders tapered to meet a tight waist and firm stomach. With symmetry and a lethally honed body, he was designed to satisfy the most insatiable.

Dressed in a pair of jeans that hugged his physique in all the wrong places, this bad boy had trouble written all over him.

He presented her with a sexy, lopsided smile. "Hey," he said, handing her a bottle of wine.

"Hey yourself." Taking a small step back, she placed the bottle on a side table, waved her hand, and gestured for him to enter. "Come in."

Without taking his eyes off her, he stepped inside. A shiver skipped down her spine at the sound of the deadbolt clicking in place.

Damn. He was so handsome. So perfect. Some deeper emotion stirred within. She moistened her lips and shrugged it off. It wasn't like she was going to fall for him if he kissed her, touched her, or made sweet love to her all night long. She knew better than to fill her head with fancy notions of love. J. C. Penney's weekend white sales were known to last longer than his relationships.

The predatory gleam in his eyes made her pulse rate kick up a notch. She began to warm in the most interesting places. She fanned her face and loosened the lapels of her robe, exposing the lace on her teddy. Was it getting hotter in here?

Schooling her expression, she banked her desires and asked, "How are you feeling? Any side effects yet?"

He shrugged, his eyes shifting downward to examine the rise and fall of her chest. A feminine thrill ran through her.

He cleared his throat and raked his bangs off his forehead. "So far, so good. I still have all my hair and I'm not drooling." His gaze roamed her body. "At least not yet," he said playfully.

She glanced at his crotch. Purely for research purposes, she told herself. "Anything going on down there?"

He grinned. "A few twitches. Nothing out of the ordinary." His eyes sparkled with mischief and something else. If she had to guess, she'd say promise. "We'll know more when we put him to the test."

She shivered with a mix of excitement and nervousness as she toyed with the belt on her housecoat. She didn't want to seem too eager, too anxious to start putting Little Jay to the test, but the promising look in his eyes prompted her into action. With renewed concentration, she plastered on an air of professionalism and fought to ignore the fine tremor of heat rippling through her.

She lowered her voice. "Perhaps we should get started. We have no idea how long this will take."

Powerful muscles shifted as he took a step closer and angled his head. His heady male scent intoxicated her and fired her senses. "Yes, perhaps we should."

Drawing a fueling breath, she inched open her housecoat, revealing a silky white chemise, lace panties, and matching garter.

A rich, decadent rumble of pleasure sounded low in his throat. Her body trembled in response. She watched his eyes darken with lust as his gaze caressed her.

Lust! In his eyes! When he looked at her!

Hot damn!

Her nipples swelled under his devouring eyes. She felt her cheeks flush from heat and desire.

His fingers bit into her hips as he pulled her hard against him. A fever rose in her when her breasts crushed into a wall of thick muscle.

His voice was husky, sensual. "How did you know?" His eyes reflected his every emotion, his every desire.

"Know what?" she rasped.

With excruciating gentleness, he skimmed her curves with his palms. "That white lace is my favorite." The deep timbre of his voice covered her like warm butter.

She cleared her throat and drew in a steadying breath. "I once read that white lace will raise any man's eyebrows."

The turbulence in his eyes made her skin grow moist and tighten. He tangled his hands through her hair and urged her mouth closer.

"Yes, well, what we're looking to raise is nowhere near my eyebrows."

She resisted the urge to scream, *Hallelujah!*

Jay watched the graceful, erotic sway of her curvy backside as she made her way into the kitchen to pour the wine. Waves of long curls cascaded down her back and bounced with each sensual movement. He smiled. It pleased him that she'd worn her hair down, the way he liked it.

He stood there, staring at her retreating back until she rounded the corner and disappeared from his line of vision. He remained motionless, unable to form a coherent thought as her exotic signature scent perfumed the air. Well, almost motionless. There was still one part of him that involuntarily twitched.

He adjusted his jeans to alleviate some of the discomfort. Christ, he knew he should have taken the time to relieve his sexual tension. Another glimpse of her curvy body covered in white lace and he was likely to go off like a Roman candle. But he'd been in too much of a damn hurry to see her to consider such matters.

A slow burn worked its way through his veins and settled deep in his groin. He'd never reacted so physically to a woman before. He couldn't understand it. Everything from her bewitching green cat eyes to her creamy flawless skin and deep silky voice aroused him.

It didn't really make a difference to him what she wore, a shapeless lab coat or a baggy robe, she still looked as sexy as hell. But hot damn, when she'd revealed her lace-clad body, the sudden need to lose himself in her became so intense it was almost painful. It took all his restraint not to grab her, bend her over, and fuck her right then. He knew it was much too soon to lose control. He wanted to take it slow, to lay her body out like a banquet so he could feast on every delicious inch of her hot naked flesh.

Ignoring his physical discomfort, he stepped farther into her roomy apartment. It was warm, inviting, and comfortable. Soft rays spilled from a corner lamp and bathed her sofa in a sensual golden glow. He grinned. That's where he wanted her. Right there. Sprawled across those plush cushions.

A raspberry candle burned near her open window. The flickering light cast shadows on the tan-colored wall while the sweet fragrance scented the air.

Raspberry. His favorite. "Mmmmm . . ." he murmured low in his throat.

He found her stereo and put on some mellow music. The kind that set the mood for seduction.

Her voice sounded from behind. When he spun around, his brain stalled. Fuck, did she know how sexy she looked when she nibbled on her lower lip like that? His nostrils flared as he drew in a ragged breath.

She stood before him, holding two glasses of wine. An erotic pink flush colored her neck.

With the crook of his finger he beckoned for her to come to him. "Come here, Laura." His voice was soft, coaxing, urging her closer.

She took three measured steps forward and handed him his glass of wine. He took a long drink, placed it on the table beside him, and angled closer until her body was only a hairbreadth away from his. He inhaled her. She smelled so damn delicious. He gazed deep into her alluring eyes, his expression letting her know this would be good. For both of them.

Jay reached out and traced the delicate curve of her jaw as he brushed his thumb across her bottom lip. Her mouth was so soft and smooth, like spun silk. His fingers traveled lower to skim her neck. An erratic pulse drummed against his touch. For a brief moment his body tightened in anticipation as he envisioned himself caressing her flesh with his lips.

He dragged his hand lower. She drew a shuddery breath when he surfed his fingertips over the milky swell of her breasts. She shifted from one leg to another, her hips bumping against his groin.

He stifled a moan and eased open the thick cotton until he glimpsed her lacy chemise.

"I really like your robe."

"Thanks."

"Now take it off."

Chapter 3

*T*ake it off.

A shiver prowled through her and she became hyper-aware of the dampness pooling in her panties. She took a moment to recapture her breath and met his challenge with one of her own.

"Tell you what, Jay. I'll strip if you do. Since we're both in this project together, I think that's only fair. Don't you agree? Besides, I'm going to have to see Little Jay so I can observe his responses."

A muscle in his jaw flexed. His nostrils flared. Jay took her glass from her fingers and set it beside his. He circled strong arms around her waist, splayed big warm hands over her back, and put his lips close to her ear. His sweet breath whispered over her nape like a lover's caress. Languorous warmth stole through her. The resulting pleasure was most exquisite.

He murmured seductively, "I knew it, Laura. Underneath that professional white lab coat, you're a rebel."

She shrugged and brushed off his comment. She knew everyone around the office called her the Ice Princess. Little did they know that deep inside she burned hotter than her Bunsen burner. It just took the right man to ignite the flame.

Jay gathered the lapels of her robe in his hands and stroked the material before cushioning her in his arms. He groaned low in his throat.

Her flesh came alive. She fought to recover her voice. "Are you game?"

"How about we take this game one step further?" He reached into his jeans and pulled out a coin. He smiled. A slow, sexy smile that curled her toes.

She slanted her head, clearly interested. "Enlighten me."

"How about we flip a coin? Whoever wins gets to call the shots. Sort of like strip poker, with a coin."

She skated her tongue over her bottom lip. Now, that was a move she hadn't anticipated. Apparently Jay hadn't gotten his "Wildman" nickname for nothing. "What are the rules of this game?"

"We each take turns flipping. You flip, I call it, and vice

versa. After each toss, whoever loses has to do whatever the other one asks." He pressed the coin into her hand. "Are you game?"

She turned the coin over in her palm and met his gaze. Her brow rose. "And this game is to test the serum? In the pursuit of science?" More like in the pursuit of seeing him naked.

"Of course."

"Well, if it's for research, then naturally I'm game." She blew a lucky breath over the silver coin and tossed it in the air. She caught it and pressed it into the back of her hand. "Call it."

"Hmmm. Heads or tails? Heads is great." He scrubbed his hand over his face as though deep in thought. "Heads is something you can really sink your teeth into, if you know what I mean." He winked playfully.

She squeezed her thighs together. Oh yeah, she knew what he meant.

"But tails, oh baby, tails works for me, too." He licked his lips and she wondered if he knew the allure of his charm.

Her breathing hitched. God, she loved his witty humor and this playful side of him.

"Call it, Jay."

He chuckled. "Tails."

Laura peeked at the coin and blew out a breath. Looked

like the luck gods weren't with her tonight. Probably because she was playing with the devil himself.

"You win."

He rubbed his hands together as his gaze left her face and roamed over her body.

His voice was low, whispery-soft. "Remove your robe."

Forging ahead, she stepped back until she reached the wall and hastily began to shrug the oversized housecoat off her shoulders.

He stilled her movements with a quick shake of his head.

She tossed him a perplexed frown. "What?"

An easy grin curved his mouth. "Slowly." He strolled over to the stereo and turned up the volume. "Feel the music, Laura. Let it guide you."

The light from the candle silhouetted his tall, muscular body. She tipped her head to look into his eyes. Her heart fluttered. He was so damn handsome.

Blocking her mind to the sudden riot of emotions rushing through her, she took a deep breath, closed her eyes, and let the music wash over her. Her hips began to undulate in time to the easy beat.

She listened to Jay's footsteps as he came back to stand before her. Her lids fluttered open. She watched him, his stance casual, his eyes tracking her every seductive movement.

She unbelted her robe and inched it open, exposing the swell of her breasts. Gracefully, she slid it down her body until it pooled at her feet. The soft cotton stroked her skin, leaving goose bumps in its wake.

When the breeze from the open window kissed her flesh, she shivered. Although she was certain the shiver had more to do with the man watching her undress than it did with the night air.

His features softened. "Are you cold?" The tenderness in his tone overwhelmed her and made her heart turn over. She looked into his eyes and saw genuine concern. This was yet another one of the qualities that had drawn her in. While working long into the night with him, she'd witnessed a side of him that was quiet and reflective, nurturing and caring. A side that not only stirred her physically, but emotionally as well.

She moistened her lips. "A little."

Jay crossed the room to close the window, then came back to stand in front of her. He trailed the backs of his fingers down her cheek.

"Comfortable now?" His tender voice chased the chill from her body. Suddenly she felt warm all over, inside and out.

She nodded. "Yes, thank you." His soft tone, gentle gaze, and intimate touch stirred her soul, filling her with warmth and unfamiliar longing.

He held his palm open and sidled closer. "My turn." He was standing so close his warm breath fanned her face. She handed him the coin and hugged herself, trying to stave off the rush of emotions surging through her.

He tossed it, stole a peek, and asked, "What's your call?" The warm masculine tenor of his voice made her shiver.

"Tails," she whispered.

Jay lifted his hand and showed her the coin. "Looks like it's your lucky day."

She wiggled her fingers at his chest. "Take off your shirt."

In one swift movement, he peeled his T-shirt off and tossed it aside. She stood there staring, slack-jawed. Her sharp intake of breath seemed to please Jay. His masculinity and virility made her tremble with need.

Jay passed the coin back to her. "You know, Laura, once I have you naked, I'm going to have my wicked way with you." His voice was dripping with desire.

Laura's throat closed as her internal temperature soared. Was he serious? Was "Wildman" Jay Cutler really interested in her? Interested in having his wicked way with her, to be precise? Was this game no longer in the pursuit of science?

Had she died and gone to heaven?

She worked to keep her voice steady. "You'll have to win a lot more tosses first."

Sexual tension hung in the air as he reached out and brushed her hair from her face. God, she loved how he touched her in such a familiar way.

"So you have no objections?" he asked.

She showed him the coin and worked past the knot in her throat. "A deal is a deal. I don't have much choice." Nor did she want one. She was both intrigued and excited by the possibility. Besides, Jay having his wicked way with her was right up there with winning the state lottery. Hell, who was she kidding? Winning the lottery paled in comparison.

She flipped the coin and won the toss. Pointing to his jeans, she said, "Take them off."

He practically ripped off his jeans and kicked them across the room.

She glanced at his shorts. Her breath stalled when she saw the huge bulge straining against the thin cotton.

Her whole body quivered in delight as her lips parted involuntarily. "Nice . . ." The word rushed from her mouth before she had time to censor herself.

"Laura?"

With reluctance, she tipped her head to look at him. "Yes?" she asked dreamily while her mind refused to tear its focus from a spot a little farther south. To think only a measly piece of cotton separated her mouth from his bulge. Mercy! Where had that delicious thought come from?

Cathryn Fox

"My turn." As though he read her every sinful thought, he smiled and leaned into her, caging her body between his muscular chest and the wall.

He took the coin from her and tossed it. Laura called it and lost. "I win," he said. A slow, sexy bad-boy grin touched his mouth and made her pulse leap. "You know, Laura, I don't need you completely naked to have my wicked way with you. The rules are you have to do what I say. That might not involve removing any clothes." He glanced at her breasts. His gaze was like a rough caress.

She shivered almost violently. It was a shiver of anticipation, not fear.

"What is it you'd like me to do?"

He cleared his throat before speaking. "Watching a woman dance really turns me on. Do you think you could dance for me?" She noted the darkening of his eyes.

She rolled her tongue around a dry mouth and began to sway to the rhythmic beat of the music. Silence ensued as she smoothed her hands down her sides and rested them on her hips. Jay's glance wandered from her mouth, to her breasts, to the apex between her thighs.

He pressed his knee deep between her legs and urged her thighs apart. His invading touch ignited her blood. "Open your legs for me." His voice was hypnotic, mesmerizing, and did magical things to her nerve endings.

She felt her nether lips inch open. Heat pooled low in

her belly and high in her loins, filling her with a restless ache. She drew a shuddery breath as her skin grew tight.

The combination of the soft light, the raspberry-scented candle, the masculine aroma of the virile male next to her, and the seductive music all played havoc on her senses. She became acutely aware of just how aroused she felt. Just how much she craved his touch. She opened her legs a bit wider.

He growled his approval.

She trembled with desire.

She took the coin from him and tossed it.

"Heads," Jay said, his voice as coarse as dry leaves. She flipped it and, without looking at it, showed it to him. "I win, Laura."

"So I guess that means I lose." Losing. Winning. It really was a fine line.

"Touch yourself."

"What?"

His nostrils flared. "I want you to touch yourself."

She touched her fingers to her throat and began a light massage.

"Lower," he said, his voice a gruff whisper.

Her hands wandered lower and lower until they grazed her cleavage. When her fingers brushed over her breasts, lust spread like wildfire through her body. Liquid moisture puddled between her open thighs.

Jay's lambent gaze washed over her like an intimate

embrace, making her forget their role-playing was for research purposes. A delicious warmth spread over her skin as she watched him carefully track her every movement. Her nipples hardened under his visual caress.

His attention drifted back to her face. "I want you to play with your breasts." His voice was a thick, rusty murmur.

Her pulse leapt in her throat and she hesitated. She'd never pleasured herself in front of anyone before.

"Put your hands on your body, Laura," he whispered. "And touch yourself." It was a command, not a request.

Her hesitation melted when his rough voice began to coax her on. A whimper sounded in her throat as unbridled desire consumed her. She'd never been so brazen before, but Jay made her feel bold. Thrusting her chest forward, she slipped her hand inside her chemise and rolled her hard nub between her fingers.

Touching her breasts fueled her hunger. She no longer wanted it to be her own hands toying with her pebbled nipples. She wanted Jay's hands palming her soft curves, exploring the pattern of her body, and extinguishing the fiery embers inside her that threatened to burn out of control.

She moistened her lips and tried to keep her breathing steady, tried to ignore the elevated thud of her pulse.

"My turn," Jay said. He flipped the coin.

Laura was desperate to win this round. So she could make him touch her. So she could feel his lips on her mouth, on her breasts, between her legs.

"Heads," she murmured as the tang of her arousal reached her nostrils.

Jay won the toss.

"Put your hand inside your panties." The deep cadence of his voice reverberated through her blood.

Drunk with desire, she did as he commanded. She needed this, needed to stroke herself, to release the pressure building inside her slick heat before her body went up in a fiery ball of flames.

Her hands skimmed her curves until she felt the lacy band on her panties. She curled the thin elastic around her finger and tugged, exposing her damp curls. She moaned low in her throat and dipped her fingers inside. The sound of Jay's harsh breathing mingled with hers. She grazed her inflamed clitoris, coaxing it out from its fleshy hood.

Forget the pursuit of science; now she was in the pursuit of an orgasm.

As she swirled her fingers through her liquid silk, she could feel the pressure building. She looked at him, her gaze pleading, begging him to help her quell the restlessness between her thighs. She ached for him in ways that left her breathless, dizzy.

His ragged voice interrupted her wanderings. "Your

turn." His breath came in a low rush. Moisture gathered on his forehead and Laura sensed he was struggling for control.

With her body beckoning his touch, she was barely able to comply. She eased her hand from her panties and reached for the coin.

"I call tails," he said as he handed it to her. It slipped from her slick fingers.

"Shit, where did it go?" Jay asked.

"It went under the sofa." Laura dropped to the floor in search of it. She crouched on her knees and bent forward. The position displayed her backside to her captive audience of one.

A growl crawled out of his throat. "Sweet Jesus, Laura. What are you doing to me?"

"It's tails." She began to wiggle out from under the sofa.

"I win," Jay said. Her body quaked as his deep, sexy voice fell over her like a bed of thick fog.

Jay pressed his hand to her back. "Stay there, Laura. I want you to stay on your knees and wiggle."

She did as he requested. When she wiggled back and forth, a jolt of fire ripped through her and she had to bite her lip to stop herself from crying out. Obviously Jay knew what he was doing. The movement stimulated her clitoris and drove her passions to new heights. If this was losing, she never wanted to win again.

As she moved her aching body against the floor, white-hot desire claimed her. She grew edgy, restless for his touch, for release. The coin slipped from her damp fingers once again and rolled out of her reach.

"Jay?"

"Yeah?"

"I lost the coin."

He dropped to his knees. "We don't need it."

"We don't?" Oh God, that must mean the potion had kicked in. She twisted around, trying to glimpse his penis.

"What are you doing, babe?" His deep masculine tenor seeped into her skin, filling her with longing.

She tried to keep her voice steady, but quickly discovered her efforts were futile. "I'm trying to see your penis. To see if the potion is working."

"My what?" She could hear the amusement in his tone.

She felt a blush suffuse her cheeks and tried to will it away. "You heard me."

"Now, what kind of talk is that? Penis."

She turned around to face him. "Well, that's what it is, isn't it?"

"Well, that's technically correct. But let's save the technical jargon for the lab. It doesn't turn me on." He leaned forward and brushed her hair from her shoulders; his gaze dropped to her exposed neck. "You know what turns me on, sweetheart?" His low, sexy voice wrapped around her like a warm blanket and she found herself inching closer.

"What?"

"Dirty talk."

Her pulse hammered. Oh boy! He had her attention. Because dirty talk turned her on, too.

"I'll start."

She nodded, repeatedly. Damn, she should have at least tried to mask her enthusiasm.

"My cock is hard and throbbing, Laura. I can't wait to fuck you."

She gulped air as her nipples quivered in heavenly bliss. Her whole body trembled as her mind relished that provocative mental image.

"Your turn," he said.

She kept her voice low, sultry. "Jay, I want to feel your cock deep inside me."

He went still. Perfectly still. Her gaze dropped to his crotch, to see if her words had the desired effect. She shoots! She scores!

In one swift movement he stood and pulled her to her feet. He pushed against her until she could feel his whole body molding to hers. His gaze was deep and intense as his heat reached out to her. For a brief moment, she thought she detected some deeper emotion flash in his eyes. Surely it was just her imagination.

In a silent message, he pushed his hips harder against her. He was hard. Rock-hard. She swallowed. He was hard and primed and hot—for her. Her pulse leapt in her throat as warm sensations moved through her.

She should have been disappointed that the serum had failed, especially since her future hinged on the success of this experiment. But, holy hell, she wasn't. She was elated.

She swallowed past the lump in her throat. Dear God, he was huge. A thrill rushed through her. Oh yeah, she was right. Not all good things come in small packages.

His mouth curved enticingly. "Then you'll have my cock deep inside you." His voice was a hoarse whisper. The turbulent heat in his eyes licked over her flesh and her body reacted with urgent demands.

His fingers bit into her hips as he anchored her to him. She shivered under his promising touch.

He lowered his head. His mouth was there. Right there. Hovering only inches from hers. All she had to do was part her lips in invitation.

That decision was taken out of her hands when his fingers began a slow climb over her curves. He smoothed her bangs from her forehead, raked his hands through her hair, and urged her mouth closer. "No more games, Laura." His voice was tangled with emotion. When she looked deep into his eyes, something special, intimate passed between them. "I need to taste you. Every inch of you." He brushed his thumb over her lips. "I'm going to start here and work my way down your body."

Overcome by his tender words and gentle hands, she liquefied under his touch.

He cupped her face and surfed his lips over her eyes, her nose, and her cheeks, before he crushed his mouth to hers and invaded with the hungry blade of his tongue. When she opened for him, he changed the angle and deepened the kiss with wild abandon.

She felt his whole body, every magnificent inch, tattooed against hers. Breasts against chest, cock against stomach, legs against legs. Laura's hands began moving of their own accord, palming the hard planes of his body, reveling in the contrasting feel of a woman's soft curves meshed against the tight rippling muscles of a man.

She writhed against him as his tongue pillaged her wanton mouth. Molten heat pulsed through her as her juices began flowing. They traded kisses for so long it left her entire body quivering.

He released her mouth and turned his attention to her breasts. His gaze skimmed her cleavage and he moaned his approval.

"You have a beautiful body, Laura."

She gazed into his candid eyes and sensed the words were spoken with conviction. *Jay liked her curvaceous body.* Warmth rushed through her and settled deep in her soul.

He dragged her straps off her shoulders, exposing the milky swell of her breasts. An erotic whimper caught in her throat. His every movement was sensual, stimulating. Her chest hammered as her puckered nipples tightened painfully.

He pulled her teddy down to her waist and took a long moment to gaze at her nakedness before he breathed a kiss over her flesh. He inhaled her skin. "You smell so good." Using tiny circular movements that drove her mad, he licked one plump bud. She threw her head back and moaned when his lips connected with her tight peaks. His wet tongue felt cool against her heated skin. God, she was drowning in pleasure. With single-minded determination, he closed his mouth over her pale mound and sucked, his teeth grazing her sensitive skin.

His hands traced her contours as they began a slow descent. His rough fingers felt delicious against her naked flesh.

Her pulse was pounding, and her soft, dewy lips opened in anticipation. The nerve endings in her clitoris screamed for attention. She became dizzy, almost overwhelmed with desire. She shuddered her surrender and widened her stance in silent invitation.

Jay reached between her thighs and in one swift movement stripped the lace from her hips. Her dark curls were
damp with passion. When he petted her drenched folds
and felt her liquid arousal, a deep, primal growl sounded in
his throat.

He brought his mouth close to hers. "You're so wet for
me, baby." There was a hungry gleam in his eyes.

He caressed her soft petals and opened her delicate pink
lips. "Tell me, Laura. Did you enjoy stroking yourself as
much as I enjoyed watching you?"

She drew a ragged breath and gathered the courage to
answer. "Yes," she admitted.

His lips brushed along her cheek. "Do you do that when
you're alone, sweetheart? Do you touch yourself?"

When she hesitated, he continued. "It's okay to admit it.
I do it, too."

"Yes," she whispered, "I like to touch myself."

"Do you make yourself come?" The soft cadence of his
tone rolled over her.

Like a bow pulled taut, she arched into him. "Yes." Her
skin grew damp, her breathing grew shallow. She'd never
been so excited before.

Her honest response seemed to please him. He rewarded
her by easing one long finger into her heated core. "Tonight, making you come will be my privilege," he assured

her, his voice full of tortured promise as his thickness pushed open the tight walls of her warm channel.

Fire licked over her thighs as his promising words nearly made her erupt on the spot.

His thumb climbed higher to stroke her fleshy clitoris. She drew a quick breath as his artful fingers worked magic.

"Tell me what you think about when you lie in bed at night and run your fingers over your body. Do you imagine it's someone else's hands caressing you?" Arousal edged his husky voice and curled around her.

She felt herself flush darker. "Yes."

"Tell me who you think of, Laura," he coaxed, his heat reaching out to her.

When she didn't answer, he withdrew his finger and purposely nudged her clitoris.

She whimpered and wiggled, trying to force him back inside, where she needed him most.

The tip of his finger breached her slick opening. "Tell me," he prodded, teasing his finger in an inch. "Tell me who you think of and I'll give you what you want."

There was something about the way he looked at her. It was as though he could see into the depths of her soul and read her every thought, her every emotion.

She gazed deep into his smoldering blue eyes and knew there was no sense in hiding the truth. "You, Jay. It's you I think of," she whispered. With that admission he growled and pushed his finger back inside.

The stab of pleasure between her legs made her breath catch. "Yes!" Her eyes slipped shut and she moaned. His finger felt so good inside her.

He found her mouth again and kissed her long and deep as his fingers kept up their gentle assault. A steady quiver erupted in her sex muscles as wave after wave began building deep inside her.

The barrage of pleasure weakened her knees. She coiled her arms around his neck and held on for fear of collapsing.

He backed her up until her legs touched the sofa. She immediately knew his intentions. She lowered herself onto the plush cushions and widened her legs, granting him entrance, letting him know in no uncertain terms what she craved.

He dropped to his knees and insinuated himself between her open thighs, his broad shoulders widening her legs. She watched his nostrils flare as he inhaled her aroused feminine scent as it saturated the room.

"Baby, you're incredible."

She raked her fingers through his hair and guided his mouth to where she needed it. "Please . . ." she begged, her heavy lids fluttering.

His tongue, teasing and tormenting, began a slow climb up her thighs. The heat of his mouth branded her quivering flesh as he approached the valley between her loins. She bucked her hips when she felt his warm breath on her nether lips. She'd never felt anything so delicious.

"Tell me you want me, sweetheart," his muffled voice came from deep between her legs.

She sucked in air as her body exploded with fiery need. "I want you, Jay," she cried out shamelessly, and fisted her hands in his long dark locks. "I've always wanted you."

She shivered with delight at the first delicious touch of his tongue. His fingers sifted through her damp curls until they contacted her sensitive cleft. With light caresses he circled her puckered nub, coaxing it to come out to play as he feasted on her. As he rained kisses over her most private parts, she began moving, pressing against him, seeking what her body craved. God, she loved what he was doing to her. Surely she'd died and gone to heaven.

"Is it good for you, Laura? Do you like this?" he whispered. His warm breath rustled her damp hairs and tickled her flesh.

It thrilled her that he was concerned about her pleasure. "Oh yes, Jay. It's good. It's never been so good," she admitted. "Please don't stop."

He pushed two thick fingers inside her, opening her wider, filling her to the hilt. The width of his fingers made her feel so deliciously full. The pleasure was almost too intense, almost too much for her to bear. He pumped into her. Hard. Fast. Changing the rhythm and tempo, bringing her closer and closer to the edge.

In no time at all, a wave of heat engulfed her. As the earth began to move beneath her, she completely came apart in his arms. She pitched against him. "Yes, that's it," she cried out, her voice choppy, rough. A sudden, powerful quake began at her core and rippled onward and outward.

Jay pressed himself against her and absorbed her tremor as she tumbled into an orgasm. Her liquid silk poured into his ravishing mouth. Stars danced before her eyes as she rode out every delicious fragment of pleasure.

He leaned back on his heels and looked deep into her eyes. When she met his gorgeous bedroom blues, a bone-deep warmth flowed through her.

He slid up her body, sank into her warm, wet mouth, and swallowed her contented sigh. She could feel his erection pressing insistently against her thigh.

She kissed him, tasting her creamy essence on his tongue. He kissed her back. It was a slow, lazy kiss that stirred her soul, tugged at her emotions, and reminded her that despite her claim not to fall for him if he kissed her, touched her, or made sweet love to her, she had done just that.

He shifted, as though attempting to keep his heavy body weight off her. That small, thoughtful gesture filled her with warmth.

"Stand up," she commanded, her throat tight with emotions.

His eyes narrowed. A frown marred his features. "Is something wrong?"

"Of course there's something wrong," she said, deadpan. He was entirely overdressed.

He gazed at her, his concern obvious in his gorgeous blue eyes. "Baby, did I hurt you?"

"No. Now stand up." She splayed her hands against his chest and pushed.

He did as she requested.

She took a moment to peruse the long length of him. "We have a problem."

"A problem?" Jay raked his damp hair from his forehead. God, he looked so adorable standing there, his eyes filled with tenderness, concern.

She curled her lips into a seductive grin. "Yes. A problem." Her gaze dropped to his crotch.

"I like your shorts."

His brows knitted together in confusion. "Thanks."

"Now take them off."

Chapter 4

"Sweet Jesus, Laura," he murmured, scrubbing his hand over his chin. The heavenly smell of her arousal lingered on his flesh and made him throb.

With a seductive gleam in her eyes, she stood up and slipped her fingers inside the band.

"Holy shit! What are you doing to me?" Sexual need made his voice husky.

Her smile stretched wickedly. "Of course, if you'd rather I didn't . . ." Her throaty purr resonated through his body. Lord almighty, if she stopped, he was certain he'd die from longing.

He rushed to get the words out. "No, no. I'd rather you did." He pulled her close and she melted all over him. Her body fit so perfectly against his. He brushed her hair from her flushed face and noted the provocative thinning of her sensuous lips.

A quick, sharp breath caught in his throat as her hand connected with his cock.

Anxious to feel her touch, he gripped the sides of his shorts and practically ripped them off. They fell to the floor and he kicked them across the room.

Panting as though he'd just run a marathon, he stood before her, his cock armed and primed like a space shuttle ready for liftoff.

She reached out and sheathed him with her palms. He immediately thickened and pulsed with desire. The feel of her warm, delicate fingers closing over his dick drove every sane thought from him. He kept his mouth clamped shut for fear of babbling like an idiot.

She idly stroked the wet tip of his arousal, then feathered her fingertips over his flesh, as though considering the texture, thickness, and length.

"I was wrong."

"You were?" Fuck! Was she having second thoughts?

"I never should have called it *Little* Jay," she murmured. Her voice grew raspy with desire.

The room began spinning on its axis. He gyrated his hips, trying to push his cock deeper into her palms. But she wouldn't let him. She pulled back slightly and watched his cock oscillate as it clamored for attention. Her slow seduction nearly undid him. His low groan gave way to a deep, throaty growl.

She leaned into him. Her thick lashes fluttered against his flesh as she began kissing a path down his throat, his chest, and lower until they were face to face, or rather, mouth to cock. Pure raw desire seared his insides.

"It's quite large."

He blew out a shaky breath. He was in agony. Total fucking agony. His juices dripped from the tip and pearled on his plump head.

Laura brushed her fingers over his slit and drizzled the liquid over his swollen sex. Heat flamed through him and he knew if she wrapped her sweet, plump lips around him, it would take every ounce of control he possessed not to explode on impact.

She made a sexy noise and shifted. "It's magnificent, really," she admitted honestly, touching him with obvious pleasure.

Christ, she was so amazing. She was everything. So wild and untamed, with a passion that matched his own. A surge of warmth flooded his veins and produced an unfamiliar fullness in his heart.

Sheathing him in her hand, she opened her mouth and brushed her pretty pink tongue over her bottom lip. "Mmmmmm."

Oh fuck. Oh fuck. Oh fuck.

Her soft moan nearly took him over the edge. Blood pounded through his cock and he felt it grow another inch. He needed to touch her, to taste her. Again and again. He reached out, stroked her breast, and pinched her hard nipple. She gasped and arched into him. Her uninhibited response brought him to new heights of arousal.

She looked up at him and lifted one perfect eyebrow. Her lips were parted. Her eyes were dark, heavy-lidded, and full of lust.

"Do you mind?"

Her warm breath fanned his engorged dick. She didn't wait for an invitation. Before he had a chance to respond, her tongue snaked out and licked a path down the length of him. He became lost in the sensation as his cock absorbed the warmth of her mouth.

His legs went weak and he nearly faltered backward. He cupped her cheeks, his hands following the movement of her head as she closed her mouth around him and sank his erection to the back of her throat.

Reaching underneath him, she sifted through the tangle of dark hair and then grasped his heavy sac. Gently cupping his balls, she gave a gentle squeeze. The erotic, silky sweep of her long chestnut curls over his thighs sent him teetering on the edge.

He threw his head back and growled. "Jesus," he cried

out, and knew that was all he could take. Sweat trickled down his forehead as a tremor ripped through him.

He gave a lusty groan and fought to hang on. He wanted to take her to bed, to make love to her properly. Slowly, passionately, all night long, but he knew he was well past the point of no return.

The tantalizing brush of her tongue as she laved the soft fold underneath his bulbous head may have brought him to his peak, but it was her soft mewling sound of pleasure that tipped him over. He tangled his fingers through her hair when he felt the pressure of an approaching orgasm.

"I'm going to come, sweetheart." He tugged her head to urge her back, but she refused to budge. She kept her mouth wrapped around him and sucked long and hard. His breath came in a ragged burst and his whole body stilled with the blinding pleasure.

Muscles straining, he shouted his release. His orgasm was so powerful and intense, his vision went fuzzy around the edges. It took a moment for him to recapture his breath and regain his bearings.

He looked down and smiled at the amazing woman kneeling before him and felt something blossoming inside him. Lacing his fingers through hers, he pulled her to his body, to his mouth.

He'd had no idea that becoming physical with her would be so moving. Laura stirred feelings in him he hadn't even known existed. In all honesty, he was unprepared for the onslaught of emotions. Somehow, during their intimate encounter, she had awakened something in him, something needy, hungry.

What the hell was going on?

Wasn't he just another "Cold-Hearted Cutler"? A man who thought only with his dick and was incapable of feelings or emotional connections with women?

She murmured deep in her throat, bringing his attention back to her. He touched her cheek. "Baby, you're amazing." He didn't even try to keep the longing from coloring his voice.

She snuggled into him and licked the moisture from her lips. "You're not so bad yourself."

He smiled and gathered her tighter in his arms. Neither said a word for a long time. They both just stood there, holding each other, listening to the soft tick of the clock in the background. Jay finally broke the comfortable silence enveloping them.

"I guess the serum failed."

"Appears that way."

He tucked a wayward curl behind her ear. "You know what that means?"

She tipped her chin to look at him and nibbled her lower lip. "Our careers are in jeopardy."

"Maybe." A spark lit his eyes. "Or we can work our

butts off tomorrow, figure out where we went wrong, and then try this again tomorrow evening."

"And if the serum fails again?"

He chuckled softly. "Then we can work our butts off in an entirely different way."

She returned his smile. "You know I'd do *anything* in the pursuit of science, but we won't be able to work until tomorrow evening. Thanks to our ever-insightful director, we have to fulfill our monthly three B's. Bonding, ball game, and barbecue."

"*By bonding outside the workplace, we accept happiness and harmony into our lives,*" they both chanted in unison.

Jay rolled his eyes. "Someone needs to tell that man we left the sixties behind us, where they belong."

"Don't let his desire for employee bonding and love for sixties décor fool you, Jay. The man is a pit bull and not to be underestimated."

He arched one brow and nodded his head in agreement. "I know, but maybe we could skip it and tell him we've already done our bonding for the month."

Laura crinkled her nose and stabbed his chest with her index finger. "I don't think this is the kind of bonding he's looking for."

Jay chuckled and anchored her hips to his. "Yeah, I guess this isn't quite the kind of employee connection he's aiming for."

"*This*," Laura said, her gaze flitting over their discarded clothes, "would get our asses canned." A smile lingered on her perfect, sensuous lips.

His thoughts scattered as his gaze dropped to her mouth. Aching to taste her sweetness and find solace in her heat once again, he lowered his head and captured her lips in a slow, simmering kiss. She opened for him, welcoming him with all the passion inside her. The velvet stroke of her tongue against his made his head ring.

Ring. Ring. Ring.

Laura broke the kiss and eased away from the circle of his arms.

He furrowed his brow. "What is it?" he asked, cupping her elbow to drag her back.

"Ringing."

He drew a labored breath. "You hear it, too?"

She grinned. "In your pants."

"There's ringing in my pants?"

Her low chuckle filled him with warmth. "Your cell phone. It's ringing."

He blinked his mind into focus. "Right." He looked around the dimly lit room. "Where in the hell are my pants?"

He followed the ringing sound until he found his jeans. He fished his phone from the pocket and hastily pressed it against his ear.

"What?" He didn't even try to keep the annoyance out of his voice.

He heard a man clear his throat. "That you, Jay?" a deep male voice asked.

Jay gave an impatient sigh. "Yeah, who's this?" he countered, pissed at the unwelcome interruption.

"It's Gerard, from Lab Security."

That got Jay's attention. He starched his spine and centered his thoughts. Lab Security calling at this time of night couldn't be a good thing. He glanced up to see Laura watching him, her expression concerned. He mouthed the words, *Lab Security*.

Gerard cleared his throat again and continued. "There's a problem down at your lab."

Jay felt his face tighten warily. "What's up?"

"It's been broken into."

Shit. Jay mumbled curses under his breath and began tugging on his pants.

"I'll contact Laura," Gerard said.

"That's okay, I'll let Laura know." With that he hung up the phone and looked into Laura's questioning eyes.

"You'll let me know what?" she asked, closing the distance between them.

A sick knot tightened his stomach. His shook his head with worry. "The lab's been broken into."

He watched the color drain from her face.

"Our research," she mumbled, her voice merely a strangled whisper.

He wrapped his arms around her and drew her close. "That's likely what they were after. Come on, we'd better get down there right away and see if anything is missing."

Laura squeezed her way between the two burly officers blocking her entrance to the lab.

One grabbed her by the arm and mumbled through a face full of donut and hot coffee. "Excuse me, miss, you can't go in there."

She opened her mouth, about to tell Detective Jelly Donut exactly where she was going and exactly where he could go, but Jay cut her off and wrapped his arms around her waist in a protective manner.

"This is Laura Manning and I'm Jay Cutler. It's our lab," he assured the officer, with a flash of his security identification card.

The officer let go of her arm, cleared a path, and waved his hand. "Oh, then by all means, come in. We've been waiting for you two. We need you to go through your files to find out what's missing."

The strong smell of ammonia assaulted her senses as Laura pushed her way past him. The sight before her left her shocked. Splaying her hand flat against her chest, she glanced at the smashed filing cabinet and gasped. The locks had been picked and files were strewn everywhere. The compilation of months of research could be lost, or even worse, stolen.

Their latest experiment was top secret for a reason. They knew if corporate-funded Ad-Tech got hold of the idea, they'd rush to produce the drug first and claim the glory, leaving Laura and Jay high and dry.

Broken vials and test tubes crunched beneath her feet as she stepped farther into the room. She carefully tried to sidestep the puddles of spilled serums.

She bent down and sorted through the tangled mess of wet papers. If the thieves had been looking for the files that recorded the chemical components in the suppressant, they'd come to the wrong place. Fortunately, those files were at her apartment. Safe and secure, under lock and key.

Jay crouched down beside her. He raked his fingers through his tousled hair and shook his head in disgust. "What a disaster." He kept his voice soft, but his anger was evident.

She shot him a sidelong glance. Tiny lines creased the corners of his blue eyes while tension lines bracketed his mouth.

"Do you think it was random?" She was anxious to hear his take on the situation.

Doubt etched his features. A muscle in his jaw flexed as he ground his back teeth together.

He must have suspected it was Ad-Tech as well. She opened her mouth to ask, but he cut off her unspoken question with an answer. Sometimes it really surprised her that he could read her so well.

"I have no doubt it was someone from Ad-Tech. This is just like something those sneaky sons of bitches would do." Gone was the tenderness she'd seen earlier in his gaze. Frustration and anger had moved in to take its place.

He glanced at her and raised his brow. "Laura—"

She already knew his question and quickly addressed his worries. "The files are safe."

He exhaled his breath of relief. "What would I do without you?"

"You might want to have a look over here," the detective's voice boomed from the other side of the small room. They both twisted around to see him standing next to the opened refrigerator. He rubbed his protruding stomach and peered inside as though searching for more jelly donuts.

Jay climbed to his feet and pulled Laura up along with him.

"This lock has also been broken. Does anything in here appear to be tampered with?" the detective asked.

Laura crossed the room, leaned forward, and examined the vials. She began a slow massage of her temples. Until she did a thorough analysis of the compounds in each and every test tube, she couldn't be certain.

"I'm not sure. It's going to take me some time to figure it out. I'll have to run some tests."

The detective handed her his card. "When you're done, you can reach me at this number."

Laura glanced at the card. Detective Jelly Donut, a.k.a. Detective Doyle. She slipped it into the back pocket of her jeans. A sound at the door drew her attention. She turned to see Erin, her assistant, standing there, her dark brown eyes wide in surprise.

"Laura, what happened? Gerard called and told me to get down here right away." Erin rushed across the room to give Laura a comforting hug.

After a quick embrace, Erin pulled back and perused the length of her. Her gaze darted from Laura to Jay and back to Laura again. "Are you two okay? You look a little flushed."

Oh boy. She might be flushed, but it had nothing to do with the break-in. "Jay and I are fine. We weren't here when it happened," Laura assured her. She waved her hand through the air. "I just can't say the same for the lab."

Erin's nutmeg-colored ponytail bounced as she glanced around. "What can I do to help?"

"I have to test the chemical components in these vials to determine whether they've been tampered with. You could help me with that."

"I'm on it." Erin saluted her, her ponytail wagging like a puppy-dog tail.

Jay came up behind Laura and brushed his hand over her arm. Goose bumps pebbled her skin. With a tip of his head he gestured toward the metal cage near the window that housed their two lab rats.

"At least Bonnie and Clyde weren't hurt." His voice caressed her flesh while his touch evoked delicious, sinful thoughts. An involuntary shudder trickled down her spine.

Laura nodded and glanced at her two favorite rats. "Now, if only our experiment had been to teach them to speak. Then they could confirm our suspicions on who did this."

Jay chuckled and brushed a curl from her forehead. His gentle touch seeped into her skin and warmed her all over. She twisted sideways so Erin wouldn't see her reaction to his nearness. The last thing she wanted was for her lab assistant to figure out what was going on. She didn't want her love life to be the topic of conversation around the water cooler tomorrow morning.

Jay pointed at the stack of papers still sitting on the floor. "I'll go through those files and try to see what's missing while you two work here."

She stared at his scrumptious retreating backside for a long, thoughtful moment. Memories of their earlier intimate encounter blazed through her mind like a firestorm. She recalled the way she'd lost herself in his arms, the way he'd brought her to heights of passion using his fingers, his mouth, and his tongue. And the way she did things to his body. Wonderful, delicious things. Things she wanted to do again and again . . .

Her toes curled beneath her as warmth gravitated to the apex of her thighs. The sound of Erin shuffling beside her pulled her back. She shook some clarity into her head, stomped down her desires, and forced herself to focus on the task at hand.

Laura grabbed a plastic clip from her desk and pinned her hair up, returning to her professional mode.

Erin leaned forward on her stool. "Um . . . what was that all about?"

"What?" Laura dipped a syringe into the first vial, squeezed a few drops into a test tube, and pressed it into Erin's hand. "Take this to the analysis lab, please."

Erin gripped the tube, but ignored her request and turned the discussion back to a topic Laura had no intentions of pursuing.

Erin's glance skirted the room and then settled back on Laura. She pitched her voice low, like they were partners in crime. "What's going on with you two?" Erin's mocha-painted lips curled like shaved chocolate.

Laura gave a quick, disgruntled shake of her head. "Nothing."

"Don't tell me *nothing*. I saw the way you were looking

at him." She narrowed her big brown eyes. "Come to think of it, you look different tonight . . ."

Laura jotted the matching vial number down in her notebook and grabbed another syringe to repeat the procedure. "I'm just stressed because of the break-in," she said, switching topics, hoping Erin would take the hint.

Erin gave her no reprieve. Suddenly her eyes went wide. "Ohmigod." Her voice raised an octave.

"What?"

"You've had sex." Her mouth dropped open.

Laura could feel heat color her cheeks. "Don't be silly. I did not."

Erin clutched Laura's arm. "With Jay." It was more of a statement than a question.

"Shh . . . I did not." She groaned and buried her face in her hands.

"Like hell you didn't." Erin shifted her lab stool closer. "Tell me. Tell me everything. I want all the juicy details. Every last drop."

"Erin, stop it, he'll hear you," she whispered, glancing Jay's way to determine if he'd heard Erin's shrieks of hysteria. She was pleased to see he was in deep conversation with the detective.

"So it is true."

Fearing her assistant was about to jump up and do the

Macarena, Laura placed her hand over Erin's and held her in place.

"Well . . . ?" Erin pressed.

Laura blew out a frustrated breath, knowing Erin wouldn't be satisfied until she knew all the intimate details. "Listen, I'll tell you everything later, if you promise to drop it for now." She hoped that was enough to appease her friend for the time being.

"Woo-hoo, I knew it. I knew it," Erin sang, rotating her arms in front of her like she was some rap singer getting a groove on.

The excitement in Erin's eyes was contagious and Laura couldn't help but grin herself. She pointed to the door. "Go. Work. We'll talk later."

Laura tried to focus on her work but easily became distracted by Jay's presence. She glanced in his direction. Standing by the window, he carefully lifted Bonnie from the cage and placed her on his palm. After a thorough examination, he brought her close to his mouth and spoke softly to her twitching nose. Emotions clogged her throat.

Laura wished she was privy to his tender words, but her distance prohibited her from hearing the private conversation. As if he felt her gaze on him, he tipped his head, lifted his eyes, and met her glance. Her heart did a little pitter-patter in her chest when their eyes locked. He smiled and gave her a sexy, knowing wink.

Embarrassed that she'd been caught staring, Laura looked down, picked up another vial, and resumed her work. A short while later, unable to help herself, she stole another peek at her handsome lab partner. He stroked Bonnie's back and then returned her to her cage. Like herself, Jay loved animals. All animals. The way he nurtured those two lab rats always filled her with warmth.

Erin came back a short while later with the results. She plopped down on the stool beside her and handed over the test tubes. "Everything is fine, Laura. There doesn't appear to be any problem with the chemical makeup of these libido enhancers."

Laura frowned. "Enhancers? These aren't enhancers. I gave you suppressants."

"Afraid not," Erin assured her. She tapped a long manicured nail on one of the vials. "These test tubes are enhancers."

Laura turned the tubes over in her hand and checked the numbers on the vials and the corresponding numbers in her notebook. Vial numbers twenty through twenty-five were suppressants, not enhancers. There had to be some kind of mistake.

"Run the test again, Erin."

Erin tossed her a perplexed frown. "Why? I already ran

them twice. There's no problem. They haven't been tampered with."

The hell they hadn't been. Those five samples were supposed to be suppressants. Unless . . . Oh no! She felt the color drain from her face. Unless somebody had been messing in her lab long before tonight.

Her stomach clenched as the truth dawned on her.

She'd given Jay a libido enhancer earlier that day, not a suppressant. She felt her blood run cold. She exhaled a quick, sharp breath and stood up. Like nails on a chalkboard, her chair scraped across the tiled floor. The sound drew Jay's attention.

"Everything okay?" he asked. In three long strides, he crossed the room to stand beside her. His gaze darted between Erin, Laura, and the test tubes she clutched in her hand.

Her mind raced with the turn of events. She closed her eyes in distress. Now it all made perfect sense to her. That was why he'd been so aroused, so eager to become physical with her. She'd known all along she wasn't his type. His erection had nothing to do with her ability to turn him on. Hell, a stiff wind would have done the trick.

Knowing that Jay could read her every expression, her every gesture, she tried to keep the disappointment from her face. She held on to her last trace of composure and settled her mouth in a grim line.

Cathryn Fox

With both Erin and Jay listening intently she focused on Jay and said, "Um, it looks like the vials had been tampered with and I gave you a libido enhancer today, not a suppressant." She placed the vials back in the tray and tried for a lighthearted laugh. It came out humorless.

A smile lit up his face. "You're kidding?"

She shook her head and squared her shoulders. "Nope."

He dropped a manila file on the counter and buried his hands deep in his pockets. The action drove his jeans lower on his hips. Laura forced her glance back to his face.

"That's great news, Laura. That means our experiment hasn't failed."

She plastered on a smile, not wanting him to know her true feelings. Of course it was good news, except for the fact that she now knew that he'd slept with her not because he wanted to, but because he needed to. She wasn't naïve enough to pretend otherwise. His hormones had been leaping like Mexican jumping beans.

She suddenly felt very chilled. She wrapped her arms around herself to stave off a shiver. He must have sensed her sudden unease.

Jay narrowed his gaze and looked at her. "You're exhausted, Laura. Let me take you home. You've been through enough tonight. A good night's sleep will clear your mind and you'll feel better."

God, she needed to get away from him, to sort through

her feelings. Carefully, she gathered up her vials, placed them inside the fridge, and fit it with a brand-new lock. Without turning back to face Jay, she tossed the words over her shoulder. "No, that's okay. I can catch a lift with Erin, she's going right by my place. We've done all we can do tonight anyway."

"Let me at least walk you two to the car."

She moved to the cabinet and pulled on the metal handles, double-checking the locks. "The police are still searching the perimeter. We'll be fine."

He walked over to her, reached out, and with gentle hands touched her cheek, drawing her attention to him. His thick muscles shifted with the easy movement. "Are you sure?"

Unable to find her voice, she nodded her assurance. Suddenly she found it most difficult to hold his stare.

"I'll stop by in the morning to pick you up for the ball game and barbecue. Then we can just head back here afterwards," he said.

"No, I'll take my own car," she rushed out. "I have a couple of errands to take care of in the morning." Shoot! She hadn't meant to sound so anxious. In an attempt to lighten the mood, she gave him a warm smile and said breezily, "I'll see you there."

"Okay. I'll stay here and clean up the rest of this mess. I'd like to run some more tests on Bonnie and Clyde again anyway and see if the latest serum works on them before we try our hand at it tomorrow night."

A shiver of unease slid down her spine. His words drummed in her head. How could she go through that again, especially after knowing what had caused his raging arousal? The reality was sobering.

Before she had time to protest, Erin jumped from the stool. "So that's what you two were up to. You tried the experiment on each other and it failed." She slapped her palm to her forehead and laughed. "That's why you ended up sleeping together, because of the mix-up in vials."

Jay opened his mouth, but Laura cut him off before he could make a sound. The last thing she wanted was to hear him confirm Erin's suspicions.

"Good night, Jay," she said, grabbing Erin by the elbow and practically dragging her out the door.

With Erin in tow, Laura pushed past the front security door and stepped outside. The cool night air helped wash away the stain of embarrassment coloring her cheeks. She ushered her very astute, but very talkative assistant across the well-lit parking lot and didn't let go of her arm until they reached the car. The horn sounded as Erin pressed the unlock button on her keypad and opened the doors. They both climbed into the front seat of her compact Honda.

As soon as the interior light clicked off and darkness enveloped them, Laura groaned and buried her face in her hands. How could she have been such a fool to believe Jay had wanted her? This was all so damn humiliating. How would she ever face him again?

"What have I gone and done?" she murmured into the palms of her hands.

"What's the big deal anyway? So you slept with the guy. Didn't you want to?" Erin slipped the keys into the ignition and started the car.

"Of course I wanted to. Who wouldn't?" She pressed her hands against her eyes and shook her head from side to side.

"True. He does tend to have that effect on women, doesn't he? I know if I had the opportunity, I'd jump his bones." She made a small slurping noise.

Laura glared at her friend and frowned intently as she pictured Erin doing the horizontal mambo with Jay. A pang of jealousy ripped through her and tilted her off balance.

"The point is, Erin, he wouldn't have slept with me if the vials hadn't gotten mixed up. You said so yourself."

Erin gave a quick shake of her head. "What makes you think he wouldn't have slept with you otherwise?"

"Because hell hasn't frozen over."

Erin chuckled. "Seriously, Laura, what makes you think he doesn't like you?"

"I'm not his type, Erin. You've seen the women he gravitates towards."

Erin adjusted her rearview mirror. "Have you looked at yourself lately? You're not in band camp anymore, Laura."

"I'm a geek magnet."

"I hardly think you're a geek magnet."

"Well, I am."

"Then Jay is the hottest geek I've ever come across."

"Just for the record, Erin, we didn't *sleep* together, we just did everything else."

Erin backed her car out of the parking space and maneuvered it onto the highway. "So, do you want to sleep with him, then? Finish what you started?"

Laura folded her hands on her lap and stared blankly at the road ahead. "No. Yes. I don't know." She rested her head against the cool glass window and sighed.

"Well, which is it, then?"

What would be the point in lying? Her expressions were so transparent. She lowered her voice. "Yes," she admitted, knowing that another night with him would be emotional suicide. Not even body armor could protect her from the way he stirred her heart.

"Then go for it. Seduce him when he comes by tomorrow night. That's what I would do."

"Hellooo. Are you missing something here, Erin? He only slept with me because the vials got switched. Besides, he's not going to want to sleep with me tomorrow because I'll be giving him a libido suppressant."

Erin lifted one eyebrow, her lips curled. "Then switch them again."

Laura's eyes opened wide in surprise at her friend's suggestion. She never would have considered doing such a thing. "I couldn't do that."

"Tsk, tsk, Laura—always the good girl. Always following the rules and coloring within the lines. Let me ask you a question. Did you enjoy yourself?"

The word *enjoy* was an understatement. "Yes."

"Did he enjoy himself?"

She recalled the heated, lustful look in his eyes. The way his body had reacted to her touch and the way he moaned in delight at the peak of his orgasm. A tremor rippled through her just thinking about it.

"I guess so."

Erin waved her hand and rushed on. "Of course he did. And he would enjoy himself again. You both would. So what's the big issue?"

Laura rolled her eyes heavenward. "The big issue? Let's try it's *immoral* . . ." She stretched out that last word. "Besides, what about the experiment? We have to present our findings to the board next week. If we don't have the results they're looking for, our grant won't be approved, and then we're out of a job. All of us. Including you," she lectured, wagging her finger to emphasize the point.

"The key words being *next week*, Laura. You still have

Cathryn Fox

plenty of time. Plenty of time to test the experiment and plenty of time to slip between the sheets with a hunk of a guy who has a reputation for fulfilling every woman's secret desire."

Laura eyed her friend. She had no doubt he could fulfill her every desire. Come to think of it, he already had.

"I didn't know you were so devious. Remind me to fire you in the morning," she said good-naturedly.

Erin grinned and pulled up in front of Laura's apartment. "Just think about it."

Laura folded her arms across her chest. "I did, and I'm not doing it," she said firmly. "Thanks for the lift, Erin. I'll see you in the morning."

"Laura, wait. Do you really have errands to run in the morning?"

"No," she admitted honestly.

"I'll swing by and pick you up for the game. There is no sense in us taking two cars when I have to drive right by here anyway."

Laura nodded in agreement. "Sounds good. I'll see you then." She climbed from the car, waved to her friend, and hurried up the walkway to her building. How on earth could Erin have suggested something so ludicrous?

She tried to push their absurd conversation to the back of her mind, but despite her efforts it kept creeping back. She pulled open the heavy glass door to the front entrance

72

and stepped inside. All she wanted to do was have a warm bath, a hot cup of tea, and crawl into bed and get a good night's sleep before tomorrow's ball game. She did not want to spend one more second thinking about doing something so devious. Because the more she thought about it, the better it sounded.

Oh hell!

Chapter 5

S till clad in her company softball uniform, Laura kicked back on a cushioned lounger in the director's private, tree-fringed backyard while she sipped ice-cold lemonade and nursed her sore elbow. She tipped her chin, drinking in the warm afternoon sun rays as the floral arrangement beside her perfumed the air and enticed her senses.

Why the director had insisted on her playing first base during the game was beyond her. Well, maybe not totally beyond her. Since everyone knew she couldn't even catch a cold with a Kleenex, playing first base gave the director and his personal handpicked team an unfair advantage. That may bring *happiness and harmony* into his life, but it sure as hell didn't bring it into hers!

Cathryn Fox

Her gaze sifted over her coworkers and settled on Jay. Moving toward her, he walked around the perimeter of the kidney-shaped pool and negotiated his way through the crowd. Gaze riveted, she appraised him as he approached. He'd changed out of his tight, ass-hugging, thigh-molding uniform and into a pair of deep blue knee-length swim shorts that rode low on his hips and exposed his athletic body. She acknowledged the sudden flare of need as her glance flitted across his face and panned down the length of him, registering every delicious detail of his bronzed skin, sculpted chest, and tight abdominals. As she devoured him from afar, a restless ache settled deep between her legs.

She brushed her tongue over her dry lips as she debated which look she preferred more, the tight softball uniform or the sexy, low-slung swim trunks. Suddenly Erin's devious suggestion to switch the vials rushed through her mind like a windstorm and caused her blood to stir. A wave of lust clawed to the surface despite her efforts to bank her desires.

Laura glanced around and noticed that she wasn't the only one taking pleasure in the view. With heat in their eyes, a few women in the pool called out for him to join them.

After he gave a quick nod of acknowledgment, his glance returned to Laura. His eyes glimmered with dark sensuality as his gaze collided with hers. Warmth and familiarity resonated through her. With long, determined strides he continued to close the gap between them.

Out of nowhere, Sue from finance pounced before him like a dog, or rather, bitch in heat, blocking his path. Lord, if the woman had a tail, it'd be wagging.

They spoke for a moment, but Laura couldn't hear the exchange over the loud volleyball game in the pool.

Head swung back, Sue's long blond hair bounced over her waify shoulders as she shared a private chuckle with Jay. Her long, lithe attributes certainly fit Jay's descriptive requirements.

The woman looked like she was waiting for him to throw her a bone. Laura's fingers clutched her drink as a strange primal possessive sound climbed out of her throat. After last night, she had an up-close-and-personal introduction to that much-coveted bone.

Laura cursed under her breath as desire segued to jealousy and pushed back the lust. It gave her a small measure of pleasure when he casually sidestepped Sue and continued his journey her way.

Jay stirred the still afternoon air as he sank to his knees beside her. She inhaled, absorbing his rich, earthy, masculine scent. When he nestled against her, a rush of moisture pooled between her thighs and gained her full attention. She shifted to face him.

His brow puckered, concern evident in his eyes. "You

okay?" The rich cadence of his voice triggered a reaction from her body. Laura lowered her head in an effort to veil her expression.

Jay cradled her arm in his most capable hands and drew it closer for a more thorough examination. It amazed her how comforted she was by his touch. Using small circles, he brushed the pad of his thumb over her skin. Oh boy! She stifled a moan of pleasure as his tender caress brought back memories of how he'd used that same erotic motion on another highly sensitive body part.

"You took a beating in that last inning."

She winced when he extended her arm.

"Ouch," she protested, putting on her best scowl, all the while hoping it would draw attention away from the way her body vibrated from his touch. "Well, you didn't have to dive for the base, you know."

Dark lashes lifted over apologetic eyes. He cocked his head. "Sorry, it was an accident." The soft tone of his voice singed her blood and curled her toes. "Of course, it wasn't an accident when I slid into second and bowled Max over."

Laura's mouth dropped open. "You're kidding?" For the last two months Max Baker, a junior research assistant from the fifth floor, had been asking her out. No matter how many times she declined, he continued to persist.

Jay's bad-boy grin turned wicked. "Nope."

"Why?"

His grin collapsed. His brows knitted together. Surely that wasn't a spark of possessiveness in his eyes. She had to be mistaken.

"It pisses me off the way he disrespects you. I know you told me you can take care of yourself, Laura." His jaw clenched and then he continued. "And I know you can, but I just wish you'd let me set him straight. He's obviously not taking the hint from you."

Her voice stalled when his blue eyes skirted over her face. His penetrating gaze robbed her of her next breath. There was no leashing the desire that moved into her stomach.

"Here, I brought you some ice." He moved closer, crowding her, and placed a cold poly bag over her elbow.

His thoughtfulness touched something deep inside her. When she glanced into his rich, seductive bedroom blues, she had to rein in her emotions. She swallowed down the raw edge of yearning and worked to keep her voice level.

She moistened her lips again and pulled in a breath, still unable to fill her lungs to their fullest.

"Thanks." Setting her drink down, she reached for the pack and anchored it in place. She graced him with a smile. "I got it." His hand grazed hers as he pulled it away. The rough caress heated her blood and aroused all her senses, leaving her warm and wanting.

And wet.

His eyes regarded her tenderly as he brushed a wayward

strand of hair from her eyes. A shiver raced down her spine.

"When that melts, let me know and I'll refill the bag."

Warmth flowed through her and touched her deepest corners. She felt an odd closeness between them as he sidled impossibly closer. There had always been an easy comfort between them, but she sensed a curious shift, some sort of unspoken intimacy with him that hadn't been there before. Maybe it was just her wishful thinking.

A sudden breeze blew through the backyard and helped cool the heat inside her. Jay remained at her side, obviously not in a hurry to *bond* with the others or to take a dip in the pool—a pool swarming with a bevy of blond piranhas just waiting for their prey.

Fearing that he'd want to discuss their botched experiment the previous evening, she guided the conversation to Bonnie and Clyde.

She arched a questioning brow. "Did the new serum work on Clyde last night?"

Once again, his brow puckered into a frown as he gave an impatient sigh. Thick muscles flexed and relaxed again as he moved himself to the foot of her lounger, gathered her feet in his hands, and draped them over his lap. He scrubbed his hand over his chin and shook his head. His square jaw clenched as he donned his professional face.

"No, dammit. That's why we really need to test it again

tonight, on me. I need to *feel* and record the results my-self." He muttered curses of frustration under his breath.

Laura, too, slipped into her professional mode and di-rected her thoughts. "I don't know Jay, I still feel something is missing from the formula. It's like we're overlooking something. Something small but vital." Deep in concentra-tion, she nibbled on her bottom lip. "I just can't seem to put my finger on it."

Bare feet padding on the cement walkway a few feet away heralded the arrival of their director and pulled her from her musings.

"Well, well, look at you two. Both deep in thought." Laura tilted her head, shaded the hot afternoon sun from her eyes, and watched Reginald Smith saunter closer.

He dipped his head. Thick gray hair, too long for a man of his stature, fell forward as his attention glided over her ice pack. "How's that elbow, Laura?"

She flexed her arm and ignored the dull ache. "It's fine. Just stiff," she assured him.

He drove his hands deep into the pockets of his tight neon-orange swimsuit that undoubtedly had been kicking around his closet since the sixties. Not a real great look for a man his age or size.

Although Reginald appeared laid back and easygoing, the look on his face spoke volumes. First and foremost, he was a businessman and not to be underestimated.

"Good. I wouldn't want that to interfere with you two presenting your findings to the board next week."

Jay's fingers slid over her bare skin and closed around her ankle. He gave a gentle squeeze. A silent message to play along. The feel of his strong hands on her naked flesh brought back heated memories of last night, making it most difficult to form a coherent thought. She suppressed a shiver, censored the provocative slide show in her mind's eye, and worked to speak.

"Nothing will interfere with our presentation," Jay said. He glanced at Laura. "Right?"

Laura tried for casual and prayed her voice didn't betray her. She gave a tight nod as they exchanged a look. "That's right," she agreed.

Reginald slanted his head and focused on Laura. "I'm assuming everything is going according to plan, then?" he inquired with an unwavering stare.

Jay squeezed again. His touch was most distracting and evoked a myriad of sinful thoughts.

She cleared her throat and centered herself. "Naturally," Laura said with much more confidence than she felt. "We've been working long and hard into the night on this."

Long and *hard* being the key words. She neglected to tell exactly *what* was long and hard.

"Of course, you both know how important the grant money is to the research center. And if all goes according to

plan, by the time next winter rolls around you can both begin preliminary trials on Pleasure Prolonged, the new serum
designed to give men prolonged erections and multiple orgasms."

They nodded in unison and then Jay redirected the conversation. "Any leads on the break-in?"

"We're still working on it." Reginald gave an angry shake
of his head as his gorgeous wife Veronica came up beside
him. "Detective Doyle seems to think it's an inside job."

Veronica puckered her pouty lips, shook her silky raven
locks off her shoulders, and slipped her slender arm around
Reginald's protruding middle.

"At least Laura was smart enough to keep the files outside the office," Reginald added.

Jay grinned at her. "That's my Laura. The brilliant one."

The brilliant one.

Not the sexy one.

Or the hot one.

Or the one he wanted to take to bed again, strip naked,
tie up, and run his tongue all over until . . . Oh boy!

Veronica piped in and helped her purify her thoughts,
jostling her back to the present.

"Come on, Reggie, you know the rules, no shop talk.
And you're needed at the barbecue," she cooed.

Reggie, as his wife so lovingly nicknamed him, draped
his arm around Veronica's shoulder, turned his back to

them, and tossed the words over his shoulder, "I expect that report on my desk before the board meeting."

When they stepped away, out of earshot, Jay leaned in and whispered, "How does a pit bull like him get a pussycat like her?"

Laura shrugged. "Beats me."

A sexy grin tugged at the corners of his mouth. "Maybe he keeps her topped up with libido enhancer," he teased. "It's amazing what that stuff will do to a person."

Laura swallowed. "Yeah, real amazing," she agreed, forcing a smile. Her stomach lurched and then growled. She knew all too well how powerful the enhancer could be. So did Jay.

"Are you hungry?"

It was as good an explanation as any for her rumbling tummy. "Yes." She jumped at the switch in subject, not wanting him to know the real reason her insides twisted.

Laura turned her attention to Erin as she opened the patio doors and stepped outside. She'd changed into a bright yellow one-piece swimsuit that accentuated her gorgeous curves. With a wave of her hand, Laura motioned for her to come over.

Jay stood and cocked a questioning brow. "The usual?" he questioned in a soft tone. "Hot dog, just mustard?"

"Yeah, thanks." Her heart tightened with his thoughtfulness. God, he was so adorable. As he walked away, he dragged her focus with him.

Erin slipped into the chair beside her. Her voice broke Laura's concentration. "How's your boyfriend?"

Laura's chin came up a notch. She gritted her teeth. "He's not my boyfriend."

"Well, you want him to be, don't you?" she teased.

Laura rolled her eyes. "What are you, twelve?"

Erin chuckled and stretched out her legs. "Heads up, Laura, crouton alert two o'clock."

Laura glanced up to see Max Baker coming her way. He adjusted his glasses and swiped his hand through puffy blond curls that reminded Laura of dandelion fluff.

"Be nice, Erin," Laura warned. "You shouldn't call people names."

Before Max reached her, the director blocked his path and engaged him in conversation. From the intent look on Reginald's face, Laura surmised it was a very important topic.

Erin shrugged. "It's not my fault he has the personality of a soggy crouton." She paused, got quiet for a moment— a rarity for her—and then as an afterthought added, "Or the breath of an open coffin." She threw her hands up in the air. "And why the hell doesn't he get a haircut? He looks like a damn chia pet."

Laura stifled a chuckle. "Erin . . . shh . . . he's going to hear you." She reached out and swatted Erin's thigh.

Erin shook her head in dismay. "I take it back, Laura."

"You take what back?"

She blew out a resigned breath. "You were right, you are a geek magnet."

Laura's lips thinned to a fine line. "You know how I hate to say I told you so." She set the ice pack aside and reached for her drink.

Leaning in, Erin whispered, "I bet all his imaginary friends have a crush on you, too."

This time Laura couldn't help but chuckle. The grin quickly fell from her face when she watched one of the piranhas climb from the pool and cuddle up with Jay as he made his way to the barbecue. The piranha's smile was as fake as processed cheese slices. Laura's stomach plummeted. The slut piranha squeezed water from her hair with her long manicured fingers and let it slide down the front of her chest in a provocative, inviting manner.

Laura didn't swing that way, but hell, the piranha even had her intrigued. Jesus, the woman looked like she could clean the flesh off a bone in mere minutes. There wasn't a guy alive that could survive a sultry strike from a man-eater like her.

An equal measure of surprise and pleasure raced through her when Jay took a small, distancing step back, regaining his personal space.

Laura tore her gaze away and whispered under her breath, "Slut piranha." She had no right to be jealous. They were simply lab partners. Nothing more. She knew what she was getting into when she agreed to be a participant in the project. Last night was just an experiment, not two lovers exchanging intimacies.

Laura wiped the beads of moisture from her forehead. "I have to get changed." Her voice came out harsher than she had intended. She swung her legs to the ground and stood up.

Erin gestured with a nod as Max weaved his way through the crowd toward her. "You better hurry before Max reaches you; otherwise, you'll never get away. By the look on his face, I'm guessing when he asks you out again, he's not going to take no for an answer this time."

Laura nodded and then stole one more look at Jay as she grabbed her duffel bag. The piranha closed the already too-small gap and looked like she was ready to sink her teeth into him.

Erin climbed to her feet and planted her hands on her hips. "Is that piranha preying on your boyfriend?"

"He's not my boyfriend," Laura quickly corrected again.

Erin ignored her and lifted one manicured brow. The devil's grin spread across her face. "You know, there's only one place for a piranha."

Laura's eyes opened wide. "You wouldn't."

"Oh no?" She angled her head. A sparkle lit her dark eyes. "Let's see."

As Laura made her way inside, she inconspicuously

kept watch out of the corner of her eye. She certainly had no right to berate Erin for acting twelve. The juvenile side of her took great pleasure in the piranha's loud shriek of hysteria moments before she made a huge splash in the pool.

Erin's voice carried over the crowd. "Forgive me, I didn't see you there," she rushed out.

Laura drew her bottom lip between her teeth, stifled a laugh, and shook her head as she made a move to step inside the house. She needed to change out of her scorching uniform and cool her heated body in the pool.

"You'd just be another notch on his bedpost, you know."

The comment came from behind and stopped her midstride.

Laura turned around and came face to face with Max. She forced a smile. "Excuse me?"

"You'd just be another notch on his bedpost," he repeated. His eyes darted from her to Jay and then back again.

Erin was right, he did have the breath of an open coffin.

Laura starched her spine and leveled a glare at him. She quickly went to Jay's defense. "I would appreciate it if you didn't talk about my lab partner like that."

Max bit back a wry grin and narrowed his beady little eyes, assessing her. "Perhaps you already are."

Anger caused her face to flush. "My love life is none of your business."

"Love?" Max asked, and let out a snort of laughter. "Is that what you think it is?"

His breath assaulted her senses and made her stomach turn. Her whole body tightened warily. She opened her mouth to refute his question, but Max cut her off.

With a derisive twist of his lips he said, "The man doesn't know how to treat a woman."

Laura turned and shot Jay a sidelong glance. She watched him prepare her hot dog. Her heart warmed with longing. Oh yeah, he knew how to treat a woman, all right. The problem was, he treated too many.

Without giving him the satisfaction of knowing he'd gotten to her, she repeated in a firm voice, "Like I said, I'd appreciate it if you didn't talk about my lab partner like that."

He ignored her and moved closer, a suggestive edge to his smile. "How about tonight, Laura? Would you like to go out? Or stay in? I could bring Chinese to your place. Or you could cook for me."

Charming.

Lord, the man was getting bolder by the day. Thank God his three-month contract expired next month and he'd be leaving. Otherwise she'd seriously threaten him with a sexual harassment complaint.

She gripped her duffel bag until her knuckles turned white. "Tonight Jay and I are working." She glanced Jay's way. As though sensing her distress, Jay caught her gaze.

The annoyed look on her face triggered a reaction from him. It amazed her how well they read each other. Jay arched a brow and took a step toward them. Laura gave a tight nod, indicating she had things under control.

Max drove his hands into his pockets. "Tomorrow, then?"

Couldn't the man take a hint? Or even a direct comment?

"Working," she replied, turning her back to him.

"I'd like to show you how a woman really should be treated," he mumbled under his breath.

She gritted her teeth, twisted back around, and added, "Just for the record, Max. I already know how a woman should be treated."

Jay had personally seen to that. Too bad she'd never again experience his gentle hands caressing her naked flesh, or his sensuous kisses on her mouth, her breasts, or between her thighs. A fine tingle played down her spine as she took pleasure in the memories.

Nope, she'd never experience such perfection again.

Unless, of course, she switched the vials.

Bloody hell!

Chapter 6

With a mustard-covered hot dog in one hand and lemonade in the other, Jay moved through the house in search of Laura. He'd seen her enter through the patio doors earlier, but she'd yet to come back out. What could be keeping her?

Unlike most of the other women at the *bonding* session, Laura wasn't the type to spend hours fussing with her appearance. He paused for a moment to realize how refreshing he found that.

Maybe she was hiding from Max. Jay felt a surge of anger rise in him. Whether Laura wanted him to or not, he resolved to take care of that guy once and for all.

Using his elbow, he knocked on the closed bathroom door. "Laura, are you in there?"

When a man's voice answered, Jay suspected she was elsewhere in the house. After a thorough search of the main floor had turned up nothing, he moved toward the staircase. Perhaps she'd gone to the upstairs bathroom to change. Since Jay had spent way too many *bonding* sessions at the house, he knew the layout like the back of his hand. He climbed the stairs two at a time, and strode down the long hallway.

He found the bathroom door ajar. With the tip of his toe he pushed on it. He opened his mouth to call out to her, but no sound vocalized as the vision before him sent his thoughts scattering in a million different directions.

Dressed in nothing but her very revealing white silky bra and matching lace panties, she was bent over the sink so enthralled in scribbling in a notepad, she hadn't even heard his approach. Her long chestnut hair fanned forward, curtaining her face, cloaking him from her line of vision.

As he stood in mute fascination, his breath rushed from his lungs. His mind raced, searching for the perfect words to describe the sensuous image before him.

He remained motionless as heated blood flowed thick and heavy through his veins. He took a long moment to gaze at her near-nakedness. Her angelic beauty floored him. His body reacted with urgent demands. God, he was so aware of her, her every breath, her every movement, her every sexy curve. Pressure brewed deep in his groin. His dry throat cracked.

Sun rays streamed through the window and spilled over her soft angles as he registered every delicious detail. With her back arched and one knee bent forward, she had her ass tipped up in the air, affording him a view of her voluptuous contours.

Sweet Mother of God!

As his dick rose to the occasion, he acknowledged just how much he loved all her soft, cushiony, womanly curves.

Everything about her stance beckoned him and bombarded his body with a primal hunger unlike anything he'd ever before experienced.

His muscles bunched.

His cock tightened.

His balls constricted.

The sudden need to feel her bare flesh beneath his fingers, to cup her perfect supple breasts in his hands, and to lick her plump nipples until she cried out in heavenly bliss made him fairly mad with longing. His mouth salivated as he recalled the silky taste of her jeweled nubs and the way they tightened under his ravishing tongue.

Every instinct urged him to take her. To bend her over

and fuck her. Right there against the bathroom counter. All night long. Lust exploded through him and dragged him under like a tsunami.

He hungered to answer the demands of his body, the needy pull in his groin. He ached to come up behind her, tug aside that scrap of lace covering her sweet pussy, and plunge his throbbing cock deep inside her tight sheath and ride her until her screams of pleasure drowned out his.

Everything in him screamed possession.

God, he wanted her. Today. Tomorrow. Next week.

Forever.

Oh fuck.

He began trembling from head to toe.

Jay cleared his throat, rattled by the foreign emotions she brought out in him. The sound gained her full attention.

She flicked him a glance but didn't bother to straighten. Dark lashes opened wide over bewitching green eyes as she acknowledged his presence.

Oh yeah, the words finally came to him. Awe-inspiring.

"Jay?"

He swallowed and softened his voice. "Yeah?"

Her eyes were alive with excitement. "I think I've figured it out."

With shaky legs, he took a measured step closer. "Figured what out?"

"The formula. I figured out what was missing."

Her soft whisper covered him like a blanket of desire, making it difficult to maintain a coherent thought. He blinked his mind into focus.

"Are you serious?"

She nodded enthusiastically.

Excited by the prospect, he said, "Show me." He came up behind her, placed her hot dog and lemonade on the counter, and glanced over her shoulder.

She threaded her fingers through her hair, grabbed her pen, and dragged it over the notebook. "When we heat compound ALD, the subcellular structure mutates. Since we need ALD to combine with the hormones for stabilization, I propose we add two cc's of synthetic PCS to the serum to help ALD maintain its structure. My hypothesis is that the molecular interaction will produce the results we're seeking."

She went still, giving him a quiet moment to absorb the information and study her theory. A slow smile curled his lips. He shook his head and marveled at her brilliance. It never failed to astonish him.

Or arouse him.

His lips twitched in total amazement. "Laura, you're brilliant."

He watched her in the vanity mirror. She dipped her head sheepishly, as though she regarded her intelligence as a personal flaw. Wisps of hair spilled down her face. He felt her shiver as he curled it around his finger and tucked it behind her ear.

Did she not understand how sexy her brilliance was?

He paused to give it further consideration. Perhaps it was time to show her.

"How did you figure this out?" he asked, studying her diagram.

She shifted, her sweet curvy ass bumping his groin. Fuck, he nearly dropped to his knees and dragged her down with him as her touch made him burn from the inside out.

Her eyes met his in the mirror. "I was standing here getting changed . . ." She squared her shoulders, and her thoughts appeared to careen off track as she suddenly became aware of her nudity. A pink hue traveled up her neck and tinged her cheeks.

Deliberately, he leaned over her, creating an instant intimacy. His bare chest molded against the smooth skin of her back. Her warm, familiar scent curled around him and filled him with longing.

He took the pen from her hand, purposely brushing his fingers over hers as he pulled it away. Circling his thumb around the button at the end of the barrel, he began to click, slowly, methodically compressing the internal spring, causing the ballpoint to pop in and out . . . in and out . . . mimicking the actions of what he'd like to do to her.

Her breath grew shallow. She moistened her lips. Her body trembled beneath his embrace. Jay sensed her mounting desire as she carefully watched him toy with her ballpoint.

Adjusting his footing, he braced his arms on the counter, caging her between his chest and the sink. Bringing his mouth close to her sensuous neck, he inhaled. He moaned against her throat, and let her rich, sensual scent stimulate his libido.

"And?" he prodded.

Her trapped body slackened against his; her voice wavered. "*And . . .*" she continued. "I was staring out the window watching the volleyball game in the pool." She paused, swallowed hard, and then continued. "The water splashed up and hit the barbecue. When it sizzled and dissipated, my mind began racing."

He moaned low in his throat. "God, I love how your mind works."

She tilted her head back. Her expressive eyes were dark and full of urgent need. The furtive brush of her curls against his cheek sent shivers skittering through him.

She gave a breathy, intimate laugh. Her dark lashes fluttered. "Really?"

"Really," he assured her. God, she was so incredible. An onslaught of emotions made his throat tighten. "Your brilliance amazes me."

Her gaze shifted back to her papers. "I see."

No, she didn't see. She really had no idea what her beautiful mind did to him. "It doesn't just amaze me, Laura."

"No?" Her smile was as shaky as her voice.

He pushed against her in a silent message, his thickening cock pressing into the small of her back.

Her breath hitched as sexual awareness arced between them. Brow puckered, Laura glanced at the open bathroom door. Jay read the unease in her body language.

In a bid to ease her discomfort, Jay inched away, shut the door, and set the lock. With slow, predatory movements he stalked back to her. Laura sucked in a tight breath as he resumed his position and pressed his cock into the small of her back once again. He circled his hands around her waist, cushioning her in his arms.

"Now no one can see us, sweetheart," he murmured into her hair. "I can do all kinds of wonderful things to your gorgeous body and no one downstairs will know." Everything about her felt so intimate, so right.

When he saw the sparkle in her eyes, he had the answer he needed. Her desires matched his. His hands skimmed her curves and climbed higher to touch her breasts, stroking the undersides through her lacy bra, hoping to make her as crazy and wild as she made him. His thumb jutted out and brushed ever so lightly over her engorged nipples. He acknowledged the way her body practically hummed.

Her fingers curled around the counter. Her cheeks took on a ruddy hue. Gone was the hesitation; in its place existed unbridled lust.

"Someone could come." Her voice lacked conviction.

He grinned. "Oh, someone is definitely going to come," he assured her. He felt her shiver at the promise in his words.

A thrill rushed through him as he watched her heated reactions in the mirror. He could feel her heart beat in a crazy cadence. He loved how she responded to him.

Fire and passion flared in her eyes. A sexy whimper sounded low in her throat. Dark hair swung back as her head lolled to the side. Jesus, he wanted her like he'd never wanted another woman before.

In a bold move, she arched her back, forcing his arousal to press harder against her ass. Once again, she met his gaze in the mirror and thinned her lips provocatively. When she looked at him with such need and desire, she made his insides quiver.

A medley of voices floated in through the open window and reached their ears.

He lowered his tone and pressed his lips close to her ear. "Don't you find it a little exciting doing it here, in the director's bathroom, with everyone outside?"

The rise and fall of her breasts drew his attention and answered his question. Raw desire seared his blood as his pulse beat in a wild rush.

Her laugh was edgy and churned with passion. "It's very naughty, Jay."

Her hypnotic voice tugged at his emotions and gained his concentration. His heart raced. He felt dizzy. Lord, he'd never dealt with these kinds of feelings before. They really threw him off balance.

The sound of her deep, sexy bedroom moan brought his attention back to her.

The room grew thick with the scent of her arousal. As he inhaled her tang, his shaft ached to plunder her, his hands ached to ravish her, his mouth ached to part her twin lips and taste her sweet feminine juices.

"Very naughty, indeed." He tucked her hair behind her ears and trailed his fingers over her silky neck.

"Tell me, Laura," he whispered into her hair. "You wouldn't happen to have a condom in that bag of yours, would you?"

"Afraid not," she murmured, her voice full of sexual frustration.

"That's okay, sweetheart, there are plenty of other things we can do."

The ice cubes in her lemonade clinked together and filled him with wild and wicked ideas. Oh yeah, there were plenty of other, *naughty* things they could do, all right.

None too gently, he grabbed her hips and spun her around to face him. His desire was reflected in her eyes. He slanted his head until his mouth was only a hairbreadth away from her. Her chestnut locks fell from their moorings and tumbled in silky waves over her slender shoulders. Their aroused scents mingled and saturated the small room.

Dragging his fingers through her hair, he angled her head and fixed his gaze on her perfect crimson lips. A fever rose in him while a thin sheen of perspiration glistened on his skin.

It took effort to speak. "How's your elbow?"

She blinked, her expression perplexed, her face flushed. "My what?" she asked, apparently confused at the sudden change in subject.

Jay chuckled softly. His chest puffed out. It astonished him that he had the ability to rattle such a brilliant mind.

"Your elbow? Is it still sore?"

"A little." She breathed the words into his mouth. His cock reacted in heated anticipation to the raw ache of lust in her voice.

He offered her a tender smile as his heart twisted. "I feel responsible for your injury." His voice sounded much deeper, even to himself.

Her pretty tongue swiped her lower lip, moistening it. She gave him a genuine smile that seeped into his soul and filled him with longing. God, she took his breath away.

Her mouth twisted. "Well, you should. You are the one

who bowled me over." Her melodic voice was colored with need and rolled over him.

Jay chuckled and brushed his knuckles over her warm cheeks. "Then maybe I should be the one to kiss it better." He traced her lips with the pad of his thumb.

She parted her plump lips, but he didn't wait for an invitation. Instead, he swallowed her responses with his mouth. A low growl sounded in his throat as his lips crashed down on hers. Hard. Possessively.

She opened for him and drew his tongue into her mouth, urging him on. Small hands reached out to touch his naked upper body. Tentatively at first, then bolder when he moaned his approval. She slid her fingers over his shoulders, down his sides, and then slipped her hand between their bodies so she could cradle his throbbing erection.

Holy fuck!

His blood raced. His heart hammered. His cock grew another inch.

Lost in the erotic sensations, Jay trailed kisses over her jaw, her neck, and lower. Jesus, her heat scorched him. He touched her all over, yet couldn't seem to get enough of her. He didn't just *want* to taste her gorgeous body. He *needed* to taste her.

Using small, determined movements, she stroked his stiff cock through his swim trunks, making it difficult to maintain a rational thought.

His knees buckled and he forced them to straighten.

"Oh God, Jay. The serum. Last night. Lingering effects." Her voice sounded broken, fractured.

She was speaking, saying something to him, but between the mad pounding of his heart, the drumming in his ears, and her choppy words, he couldn't comprehend anything.

In his haze of lust it took all his effort not to tear her sexy panties off and have his wicked way with her. Before he gave in to such indulgence, he needed to slow down, to do this right.

For her.

Jay shook the buzz from his head, took deep gulping breaths, and worked to maintain what little control he had left before it was completely obliterated.

He sank to his knees, skimmed his fingers over her sleek bare legs, and then wrapped his hands around her waist, holding her tight against him as he breathed in her scent.

He glanced up at her and drew a fueling breath. "Does it hurt anywhere else, Laura?"

Sagging against him, she gave a quick nod and skated her hands over his flesh, brushing his hair from his face. Moisture pebbled their skin, melding their bodies as one.

He became unhinged as her eyes moved over his body and caressed him with sultry heat. A fine tremor rippled down his spine.

He closed his eyes against the flood of emotions.

"Show me, and I'll kiss it better." His voice dropped an octave.

Green eyes darkened and burned with lust. Her breath came in a ragged burst. "I ache here." Her sweet scented breath fanned his face as she exhaled. Hands shaking, she cupped her full breasts in offering. Her fingers surfed over her puckered buds as though attempting to relieve the ache.

Sweet Jesus! Pleasure engulfed him. Jay shackled her hands and anchored them to her sides as his mouth found her hard, distended nipple. He kissed her and brushed his tongue over one engorged pebble through the silky fabric. Using his teeth he nipped her material and tucked it under her breast, freeing her mounds from their constrictive confines.

"So beautiful." He blew a warm breath over her quivering flesh.

"Oh, Jay," she whispered, arching into his mouth. The fire in her eyes licked him from head to toe.

He growled and began lapping at her with hungry strokes, greedily pulling her taut nipple between his teeth, sucking, nibbling, and relishing the taste until her moans of pleasure merged with his. Turning his attention to her other breast, he treated it to the same tongue bath. God, he loved how they swelled in his mouth.

As though in a bid to ease another deep ache inside her,

she rubbed her sex against him. The movement was slight, but it hadn't gone unnoticed.

He glanced up at her and raised a brow. "Does it hurt somewhere else, Laura?"

Her chest rose and fell in an erratic pattern, her breath sounding labored. She blinked. "Yes," she admitted.

Jay inched back and rested his hands on her hips. "Touch yourself, Laura. Touch yourself and show me exactly where it hurts," he commanded in a gentle voice.

Without pause, Laura trailed her hands over her body until she reached the apex of her legs. "Here, Jay. It hurts here." He heard the impatience, the need in her voice.

It thrilled him, the way she played along. Warmth settled low in his gut as everything in him reached out to her. She did strange things to his insides. Foreign emotions pressed against his heart, causing it to tighten.

He took a fortifying breath and worked to keep his voice level. "Would you like me to kiss it better?"

He watched her throat as she swallowed. Her legs widened involuntarily. "Oh yes . . ." came her breathy reply. "I would definitely like for you to kiss it better." Her dark lashes fluttered shut.

Seeing her this excited made his body pulse and throb in sweet agony. His muscles clenched with the tension of an orgasm.

He curled his fingers around the lacy scrap of material

and tugged it aside, exposing her sweet sex. Leaning in, he inhaled her aroused scent. His nostrils flared. The intensity of his desire for her was most frightening.

He pulled open her dewy lips for a closer examination. "Oh yes, Laura. I can see that you ache here." With a feathery light caress, his thumb circled her clit. It was hard, inflamed. "You're very swollen."

Laura trembled and quivered under his touch. "Please make the ache go away," she begged.

"Oh, I plan to, sweetheart." He pressed a kiss over her drenched mound and parted her folds with his tongue. Her juices began to flow. The first delicious taste pushed him to the edge.

"Is this helping?" he asked as he made a slow pass with his tongue, hoping to make her delirious with pleasure.

She spread her legs wider, granting him deeper access. "Not yet, you better keep trying . . ." When he kissed her again, her voice fell off as a moan worked its way up her throat.

He deepened the kiss and then slipped one finger inside her tight fissure. A heated moan tore from her throat. When he felt her slick heat, pleasure forked through him and tilted his world off its axis.

He drew a quick breath and glanced up at her. His voice thinned to a whisper. "Laura, you're dripping." Did she have any idea what that did to him?

Torrid heat filled her seductive eyes when they met his. She whimpered and bucked against his hand. "You make me this way."

Jay pushed another finger in and swirled it around her liquid heat. She grew slicker with each stroke.

"Does this help, Laura?" he asked as he dipped into her syrupy arousal with the soft blade of his tongue and curled it around her clit. "Does this help the ache?"

Her whole body vibrated. It amazed him how much pleasure he took in pleasuring her.

"Ohmigod," she murmured as he applied the perfect amount of pressure to her beaded pearl. He could tell she was close by the way her muscles clenched around his fingers and sucked him in deeper.

"Does it still hurt, Laura?" His body ached to join with the heat between her legs.

She pulled in a breath, writhed and moaned. "Yes." Her deep, raspy voice made his cock pulse.

He frowned in concentration. "Then perhaps I've been doing this all wrong. Maybe I need to change tactics."

She raced her fingers through his hair, gripped his head, and pinned his mouth to her sex. "Oh no, Jay, you've been doing it all right," she rushed out. "It's helping ease the ache. Please don't stop."

With determined strokes, he worked his finger in and out of her while his thumb spiraled higher to toy with her clit. She bucked forward, impaling herself on him. He changed the rhythm and tempo and stroked her G-spot until she convulsed in his arms. Moments before he allowed her to tumble into orgasm, he inched his finger out and slathered her creamy essence over her clitoris in a slow massage.

"Jay . . . no . . . please." Her shameless begging thrilled him.

He chuckled easily. "I think I may need to ice it."

Her eyes flew open. "Oh God," she cried out, her hands clutching the edge of the counter.

Without breaking eye contact, Jay gripped the thin elastic straps on her panties and, in one fluid motion, snapped them.

Laura gasped in surprise. Jay tossed the scrap of material aside and reached for her lemonade. He took a slug, fished out one ice cube, and set the plastic cup back on the counter.

"Have you ever used ice to take down the swelling before, Laura?" he questioned softly.

She gave a quick shake of her head. Her eyes were alive with eager anticipation.

Good. He wanted to be the first. Come to think of it, he wanted to be the first for a lot of things where Laura was concerned.

"Let's see if this helps, then." He breathed the words over her pussy and watched her damp hairs bristle.

Goose bumps pebbled her flesh when he touched the ice to her skin. Their eyes met and locked as he trailed it over her stomach and higher. He feathered it over her supple breasts and slowly circled her hard nipples. Her buds puckered and throbbed as he brushed them with ice. In no time at all, the ice began to melt against her scorching body.

Hands trembling, she began to shake almost violently. "I don't think it's working, Jay. It's making me ache more," she whimpered, and touched her body all over.

With a tap of his hand, he urged her thighs farther apart. "Maybe I'm not touching the right spot." Her eyes opened wider when he put a fresh cube between his lips and dipped his head.

As he sank his mouth into her warm, wet, passion-drenched heat, he manipulated her clit with the frozen cube. Her skin tightened and quivered under his gentle assault. As he plucked her inflamed pearl, he probed her opening with his finger, bringing her closer and closer to the edge of ecstasy yet never allowing her to tumble over.

She began clawing at him. A cry lodged in her throat. Her body shuddered uncontrollably against his invading mouth.

"Jay, I'm so close. Please, I need to come." She gyrated against him.

He was drowning, losing himself in her sweetness. His cock ached so hard now, juices dripped from the slit. It took everything in him not to reach inside his shorts and stroke himself.

When the cold ice turned to liquid, he replaced it with his tongue and pushed another finger inside her. His burning mouth pressed hungrily into her heat. She palmed his muscles and squeezed her legs together, her silky thighs hugging his face.

He breached her opening with a third finger. "Would you like another?" Barely able to draw air into his lungs, he breathed the words over her pussy.

"Yes . . ." she hissed.

Deciding to end her sweet torment, he changed his small quick laps into long luxurious strokes. He pushed his third finger all the way in, filling her to the hilt. It was a deliciously snug fit. Slowly, he pumped his fingers in and out. She began to shake with sexual frustration. When he increased the tempo, he felt her body go up in flames.

With unabashed passion, she began moving, pressing against his mouth, eagerly riding his fingers, driving them in deeper. She knew what she needed to take her over the edge and she was damned well determined to get it. He loved that about her.

"Jay . . ." She whispered his name and dragged her hands through his hair as her body began to quake and tremble with pent-up need. She rode him furiously, with fierce intensity. Her sex began to tighten and contract.

When he felt the first erotic pulse of her release, his mouth curved. He gave a low growl of satisfaction. "That's it, Laura. Let it go. Come for me."

Her eyes flashed like lightning. "I . . ." That one word spoke volumes.

"I know, baby . . . I know."

Her skin came alive as her pussy muscles undulated. Panting hard, she shuddered and gripped his head for support as a powerful orgasm tore through her. Her syrupy release dripped languidly over his ravishing mouth. He lapped at her milky sweet climax and held her tight as she rode every delicious wave of pleasure. A moment later her contented sigh of pleasure filled the small room.

God, she was so damn sexy. A rush of tenderness washed over him as he watched her succumb to her needs and give herself over to her orgasm.

Jay's cock throbbed as he climbed to his feet, gathered her face in his palms, and looked deep into her sated eyes before he pressed a kiss over her mouth.

"Mmmm," he moaned. "Laura, I've never tasted anything sweeter."

She took deep gulping breaths and rested her head against his chest. He raked his fingers through her hair and held her until her breathing returned to normal.

As he held her close, he fought valiantly to suppress his arousal. Lord knows he was going to have to usher Laura out of the bathroom so he could take care of that huge problem before he went back outside. There was no way he could join in the bonding session in such an obvious state. He knew it wouldn't take long to relieve himself. Christ, he was so aroused, after a couple of quick strokes he'd be done.

Laura thrust her hips forward and bumped his swollen dick. A low groan of longing crawled up his throat. When he met her glance, a mischievous grin curled her lips.

"I'm thirsty." She inched back, grabbed her lemonade, took a long swallow, and drew an ice cube into her mouth. Swirling it over her tongue, she pushed Jay backward and glanced pointedly at his crotch.

His voice was thick with desire. "Laura?"

"Hmmm?" Her gaze turned heated. With just one smoldering look, he knew her intentions.

His pulse kicked into high gear.

"Jay, you look like you might have gotten hurt when you slid into first base. You look a little swollen yourself. I think we need to apply ice."

Sweet mother of God!

Her hands milked his rock-hard cock as she leaned into him and pressed her lips to his mouth. He drew her cold, lemonade soaked tongue in for a more thorough taste. A moment later she inched back and sank to the floor. She positioned herself between his legs and snuggled in closer. With her eyes latched on his, she slowly tugged his swimsuit to his ankles. His huge boner sprang free and gained her full attention.

She stared at his cock in frank appreciation. "So lovely." Her eyes widened in pleasure as she paused for a brief moment to take in the sight of his phallus.

"Oh yes, I can tell you ache here." She ran her forefinger down the length of his shaft and shook her head. As she caressed him, his cock darkened and throbbed beneath her fingertips.

"I'm afraid it's much worse than I thought." A bemused expression crossed her face.

Lust hit him tenfold. He took deep, shallow breaths and grabbed for the towel bar to balance himself before his rubbery knees sent him crashing to the floor.

"I think not-so-little-Jay is going to need extra-special attention to help reduce *this* kind of swelling."

Arching into him, she brushed his cock with her ice-soaked, cold velvet tongue.

His body tensed.

His dick jerked upward.

His semen raced to the finish line.

Oh shit!

Her voice was a low velvet murmur and ignited his blood to near boiling. "Oh yes, after I apply ice, I'm definitely going to have to kiss you better. It's very, very swollen. In fact, it's turning purple," she teased. Her pink tongue snaked out and caressed the tip.

His cock glistened where her tongue had trailed a path. His breath came in a low rush as flames surged through him. He pulled his hand from the towel bar, smoothed her hair from her face, and gyrated forward. Her soft mewl played over his flesh as she dipped her tongue into the liquid arousal dripping from his tip.

"Laura, you're damn near killing me." Desire deepened his voice. "I can barely stand."

She grinned. "Then you'd better hang on to something." She popped another ice cube into her mouth and sank his cock to the back of her throat. She ran the cold cube over the tip of his dick until he quaked. Giving him reprieve, she replaced it with her warm lips. The hot-cold medley blew his mind.

She was so damn sexy. So damn hot. So playful. So brilliant. So . . . so everything . . .

Her delicate hand slipped between his legs to cradle his balls. "Does it hurt here, too, Jay?" she asked, blinking up at him with wide-eyed innocence.

"God, yes," he growled.

Smiling, she drew his dick back into her mouth. The

sight of her plump lips curled around his cock as she plunged forward weakened his knees. Oh man, she was so good at this.

He fisted her hair in sweet agony as he fought to hang on. Christ, he barely even made it out of the starting gate and he was already reaching the finish line. This was not going to be one of his finer moments.

"Laura, I'm not going to last." His voice sounded tortured.

Her sweet, erotic moans of ecstasy made him quake. Her tongue swirled around his engorged head while she sucked harder, drawing his climax. Soon the ice melted and her mouth seared his sensitive flesh.

Bucking forward, he drove his cock in deeper as his thickness pulled her gorgeous lips apart. She rocked on her heels as he pumped into her with fervid passion. His whole body trembled and tightened with the onset of release.

She glanced up at him. The desire reflecting in her eyes became his undoing.

Laura caressed his sac and he knew his time had come. Lord almighty! Someone stick a fork in him, he was done. His muscles spasmed as she sucked him in deeper, urging him on.

Throwing his head back, he growled like a wild animal. He felt an explosion of his senses as he shot his liquid heat down her throat.

Laura rested her head against his thighs and remained between his legs for a long time. Once his breathing became more regular, he reached for her and pulled her to her feet. She smiled when their eyes met. He tucked her hair behind her ears and dropped a soft kiss onto her mouth. She gave a quiet sigh and snuggled in tighter.

As he looked deep into her eyes, his heart filled with emotions. Being with Laura and making love to her with his mouth and hands had washed away the memories of every other woman he'd ever been with.

Understanding dawned in small increments. For the first time in his life, a woman had penetrated his heart and touched him on a whole different level.

He paused to consider that further. Maybe he wasn't just another "Cold-Hearted Cutler." Maybe he was different from the other men in his family. Maybe it just took the right woman to open his eyes and prove that he was capable of love. He shelved those thoughts to examine in depth later.

He tightened his embrace, needing to hold on to her a bit longer.

A sound outside the bathroom door reached his ears.

"Laura."

"Yeah?" Her voice sounded drowsy.

"Someone's coming."

She grinned playfully. "Haven't we already been through that?"

He slid his finger under her chin and lifted until their eyes locked. He jerked his head toward the door. "No, Laura, really, someone is coming."

Chapter 7

Startled, Laura darted a glance from the closed door, to Jay, to her duffel bag, which lay just out of reach. The sound of footsteps grew closer, then stopped outside the bathroom.

Oh God.

Way to go, Laura, she thought. Having sex with your lab partner in the boss's bathroom is one hell of a career move.

What in the heck was it about Jay that made her so bold, made her take so many risks?

He reached for her duffel bag and placed it on the counter. "Quick, get dressed," he whispered as he tugged on his swim trunks and scooped her torn panties off the floor.

With shaky hands, Laura rifled through her bag and

pulled out her bathing suit. A soft tap on the door caused her movements to still.

In a silent message to Jay, she pressed her finger to her lips. He nodded in understanding.

She cleared her throat. "Someone is in here," she called out.

"Laura, is that you?"

She swallowed at the sound of Veronica's voice.

"I'm just getting changed. The downstairs bathroom was occupied."

"No problem, hon. Reggie asked me to find you, he wants to know if you'll be on his team for the water relay races."

So *now* he wanted her on his team. All because she was a damn great swimmer. The man played to win. Happiness and harmony, her ass!

"Okay, I'll be down in a sec." She hated how shaky she sounded.

"Have you seen Jay?"

"No," she replied much too quickly.

For a moment Veronica went silent. "Okay. If you see him, tell him Reggie wants him, too."

"I will."

"I'll see you downstairs, then."

Laura closed her eyes, let out a breath, and then hastily tugged on her one-piece black bathing suit and wrapped her matching sarong around her flared hips. She noted the way Jay's eyes fixated on her supple curves. A feminine thrill ran through her. The way he looked at her with eyes imbued with desire made her feel as though she were the most beautiful woman alive, and for the first time in her life she was elated with her above-average IQ.

"Oh, and Jay?" Veronica said.

"Yeah?" he asked, automatically responding to his name.

Laura's eyes sprang open, her mouth widened in a silent gasp.

He winced. "Shit," Jay whispered, smacking his palm to his forehead.

Veronica's chuckle reached their ears. "You might want to shut the window next time."

Laura's heart nearly failed. Heat colored her skin from head to toe.

"Fuck." Jay cursed under his breath and scrubbed his hand over his jaw.

Before either could respond, Veronica rushed on, "Don't worry, I was the only one sitting below your window, so I'm the only one who heard your . . . uh . . . your research."

Laura finished dressing and threw her ball uniform into her duffel bag. "We better get out of here before anyone else takes an interest in our *research*."

By the time they dressed and made it downstairs, the water relay games had already begun without them. For that, Laura was pleased. Her mind was too preoccupied to partake in any of the *bonding* activities. Besides, as it stood, she'd already done enough employee bonding for the day. Just not the kind the director approved of.

Laura glanced around, fretting that her coworkers, and especially her ever-astute assistant, Erin, would suspect the pink hue on her cheeks had nothing to do with the late afternoon sun.

Standing poolside, Jay turned to her. "Let's get out of here, Laura. I'm anxious to head back to the lab and test your theory." His handsome face was eager, the way it always was when they were on the heels of completion. God, she loved his enthusiasm and his single-minded determination. She loved that his ambitions matched her own.

Laura shaded her eyes. Her gaze skirted the crowd in search of Erin.

Jay read her body language. His voice softened. "Come with me. We'll go to the lab together and I'll run you home later. With the director breathing down our backs, the sooner we get this perfected, the better." He stood so close his warm breath fanned her face. Snaking his hand around her back in a protective manner, he played with the tendrils of hair at her neckline.

God . . . when he touched her like that, like he really meant it . . . She shivered as his tender caress stirred all her emotions.

Deep inside she knew she should have put a stop to their

intimate play, knowing what had caused his raging arousal, but damned if she could bring herself to do it. Lust overshadowed sensibility, leaving her powerless to control her desires.

Laura drew a fortifying breath. Needing time to regroup before they worked late into the night, she said, "You go ahead and get started. I'm going to get a lift with Erin. I don't have any clothes with me and I need to go home and change first."

He shook his head. His jaw clenched. She knew him well enough to know he was about to voice an argument and urge her to change into a pair of scrubs at the lab.

She arched one brow playfully. "I need to get some panties," she whispered. "Mine are ripped."

He grinned, a glint of humor in his eyes. "I'll replace them," he promised sheepishly. She sensed his resolve melting.

"I'll meet you there," she insisted, not giving him time to protest.

He rolled his shoulders. "All right. Don't be long. This is going to be great."

Excitement danced in his eyes and pulled Laura in. Like her, Jay really loved this aspect of their job.

Laura searched through the now-dwindling crowd and found Erin sprawled on a lounge chair. She hurried her steps over to her.

"Hey," Laura said. "Ready to get out of here?"

"Where have you been?" Erin asked, stifling a yawn. "I've been ready for an hour."

An hour? Surely she and Jay hadn't spent an hour in the bathroom.

"Let's go." Laura held her arm out.

Erin accepted the offered hand and let Laura pull her to her feet. As Erin stood, her gaze slowly, knowingly drifted over Laura.

Erin braced her hands on her hips, a grin tugging her lips up. "Now it's my turn to say I told you so."

Laura didn't even bother to mask her feelings. After all, her emotions were as transparent as cling wrap. "And . . ." she said, turning on the ball of her foot, "I know you're just dying to elaborate on that statement."

Erin fell in step with Laura as they exited the backyard through the gated fence and made their way to Erin's car.

Erin lowered her voice. "Last night I told you Jay slept with you because he liked you, not because of the enhancer."

Laura pulled the car door open, paused, and glanced at Erin over the roof. She lowered her voice to match Erin's. "Tell me something, Erin. You were there months ago when we tested the enhancer. How long did it stay in a man's system?"

Erin gave her a look suggesting she was crazy and cut her hands through the air. "I don't buy that for a minute." With a nod she gestured toward the backyard. "Even if it was still in his system, which I doubt, he could have had his pick of any piranha in the place, and he chose you." Her grin turned wicked. "The guy's got it bad for you."

Laura's heart kicked up a notch as Erin's words sank in. True, the effects usually lingered for a little over twelve hours, and they were well past that. And he could have had any slut piranha in the place. That was blatantly obvious.

Could Erin be right?

Could Jay have it *bad for her*?

Had hell frozen over?

Laura climbed into the car and secured her duffel bag at her feet. The strong smell of Erin's pine-scented car freshener assaulted her senses and made her sneeze.

Erin turned to face her. "So tell me, did you finally get to finish what you started? Was he as great as I hear?"

Heat climbed to Laura's cheeks as jealousy surged up inside her. She really hated thinking about Jay being *great* with other women.

"No." Laura cracked her window and drew a breath.

Erin leaned forward, her dark eyes wide in disbelief. "No? He wasn't great? Or no, you didn't finish what you started?"

"I wouldn't use the word *great*, Erin. It was more like

amazing, mind-blowing, and earth-shattering. And no, we didn't finish what we started." Laura shrugged. "No condoms."

An impatient sigh filled the car. "Girl, have you learned nothing from me?" She reached into her dash and grabbed a handful of super-sized prophylactics and dangled them in front of Laura.

Erin raised an inquisitive brow. "I take it he needs extra-large?" she inquired hopefully.

Laura gave a tight nod and swallowed as she recalled his magnificent girth. "Oh yeah," she squeaked out, and linked her hands together.

Erin grinned. "If you want him again, and if you want to finish what you started, seduce him. That's what I'd do." She stuffed the condoms in Laura's bag. "And keep a stash of these with you at all times. You never know what might *pop* up."

A short while later, after Erin had dropped her off at her building, Laura made her way inside. As she pulled open the security door, her thoughts returned to Jay. Heck, who was she kidding, her thoughts didn't *return* to Jay, they had never left him.

God, she couldn't believe that they'd ravished each other like that in the director's bathroom. Nor could she believe the erotic, stimulating things they did with the ice cubes. She'd never been so bold, so daring, so naughty. Or so reckless.

Even though the sex was fantastic, the more time she spent in Jay's arms, the deeper her emotions spiraled out of control. And to think they had to test the suppressant again. A shiver made its way down her spine.

Jay had said her brilliance amazed him. In fact, he said it did more than just amaze him, and proved that fact to her in orgasmic ways. For a moment Laura pondered the situation. Was Erin right? Did Jay have it bad for her or was it the libido enhancer ruling his actions?

Suddenly Max's words came back to haunt her. *"You'd just be another notch on his bedpost."*

Even if Jay did find her attractive, he was a playboy—a renowned playboy who wasn't searching for anything more than a wild time.

They simply slept together. Lots of people slept together and it didn't mean they were in love. She swallowed the knot in her throat and pushed those thoughts to the far corners of her mind.

Exhaustion settled into her bones as she climbed the stairs to her apartment. She'd like nothing more than to go to bed and crash for a week but she knew she couldn't go to sleep yet. She had to meet Jay at the lab to test her theory.

Just as she prepared to put her key into the lock, she noticed her door was ajar. She straightened in surprise. Had she forgotten to lock it earlier that morning in her haste to make it to that ball game?

When she inched the door open and peered inside, blackness greeted her. Taking one tiny step, she reached for the light switch. Glass crunched beneath her feet. Her heart lurched in her chest and her thoughts raced as air rushed from her lungs in a loud whoosh.

Before she had time to quietly tiptoe out of there, someone, a very big someone, came barreling into the hallway, knocking her backward. Her head hit the wall and her legs went out from underneath her. She winced in pain as she crumpled to the floor.

The intruder's footsteps pounded down the hallway like thunder as he bolted down the stairwell and out the main door.

It took her a few minutes to pull herself together and gather the strength to rise. Crawling to her feet, Laura stood there, blinking, dazed, trying to figure out what in the heck had just happened.

Erin's voice sounded from behind. Laura spun around. The quick movement made her dizzy.

"Whoa," she mumbled, groping for the wall to right herself.

Erin put her arm around Laura's waist and balanced her. "Laura, what happened? I saw a man running from the building."

"Call Detective Doyle; his card is on my counter. I think I just ran into the guy who broke into the lab."

*   *   *

Jay hurried to the research center, grabbed a quick shower in their lab changing room, and dressed in a spare pair of jeans and T-shirt that he kept stashed in his locker. He spent the next hour carefully preparing and heating the new compound. Once completed, he filled a syringe and administered the shot to Clyde. Ever since he'd given the rat an enhancer fifteen minutes earlier, the little guy had been stalking around his cage like a wild panther in search of Bonnie, in search of relief. He knew the feeling well.

Although he had to admit, his sleeping with Laura the previous night had nothing to do with the libido enhancer surging through his body. Oh no. Not at all. He'd slept with Laura because he was damn well crazy about her. What he experienced with her, inside the bedroom and out, was unique, extraordinary, something he'd never experienced with another woman. Or ever would.

He loved everything about her. Her beautiful face, hair, and body. He even found the way she nibbled on her bottom lip endearing. He loved her spirited energy and dedication to her work. He loved her sense of adventure and how she had maintained her humor at the ball game, even when she got bowled over. A low chuckle sounded in his throat. Talk about taking one for the team. Jay especially loved her intelligence. Not only did she arouse his libido, she stimulated his mind. No other woman had ever done that.

Realization dawned. The deeper emotions he felt with Laura proved he wasn't incapable of love, like he'd thought, like he'd always been told. It wasn't that he was a total Cutler clone. Not at all. It was simply that the right woman had never come along and opened his heart.

The significance of his thoughts didn't elude him.

It never occurred to him that in his original quest to melt the Ice Princess he'd stumbled onto something he had no idea how much he wanted.

Now that he'd found it, it made him rethink his lifestyle, his future. Until tonight, he'd never really known how lonely he'd been. How tired he was of the bachelor lifestyle, tired of going home to an empty apartment, eating alone, waking up alone.

He'd never brought a woman to his place before. It was much less complicated to spend the night at hers, and then escape when the time was right.

For the first time in his life, he wanted to bring someone into his home, his territory. He longed to wake up next to a woman who was sweet and caring, warm and welcoming. He wanted to feel Laura's loving body in his arms, to kiss her awake and spend the weekend talking over coffee. He wanted to share her happiness, her heartache.

The night they'd spent together at her apartment certainly hadn't satiated his appetite for her, the way he thought it would. In fact, his reactions were quite the opposite. It left him wanting, yearning for more. So much so that he ravished her in the director's bathroom. He was losing himself in her. Body and soul.

It basically boiled down to one thing. He wanted Laura, inside the bedroom and out.

He could tell her how he felt, but why would she believe him? He knew his reputation as a playboy preceded him. No doubt she'd assume he was sweet-talking his way into her panties again. Not that he didn't want her writhing between the sheets, mind you. He did. After all, he was a healthy red-blooded male.

But that would have to wait, because right now he wanted to show Laura there was more to him. To show her how much he cared, how he longed to be with her, and how good they would be together outside the bedroom. He wanted to prove to her that he was worthy.

He turned his attention to Clyde and watched him run laps inside his exercise wheel in an attempt to burn off some of that excess steam. "Ease up there, little buddy, before you hurt yourself."

Reaching into a nearby cage, he gathered Bonnie into his hands and brought her close to his face. He murmured into her ear. "Hopefully the potion works this time and Clyde will give you a break." Bonnie's nose twitched as she wiggled to free herself.

He placed Bonnie into the far side of the cage and

waited. Clyde stopped spinning his wheel, went up on his hind legs, and sniffed the air.

Jay scrubbed his hand over the prickly growth speckling his chin and observed Clyde's actions. He glanced at the clock and yawned. What was taking Laura so long?

Clyde stopped sniffing, climbed from the wheel, circled like a cat, and then curled up in the fetal position. In no time at all he fell fast asleep. A wide grin split across Jay's face, but he was too damn tired to jump up and down with excitement. In an automatic reaction, he turned to tell Laura the good news but quickly realized she wasn't there. A sense of loneliness enveloped him. It surprised him how he'd grown so accustomed to having her at his side.

As he made his way over to his desk to note his findings, his cell phone vibrated and began ringing.

Who would be calling at this time of night? He dug into his pocket and flipped open his phone. Perhaps it was Laura letting him know she was running late.

"Hello."

"Jay, it's Erin." She sounded anxious.

He froze midstride. "What's up?"

"You better get to Laura's place right away. Her apartment's been broken into and she's hurt."

His whole body stiffened. Laura was hurt. How? Where? Who? Before he had time to ask any of those questions, Erin hung up.

Dropping everything, Jay bolted out of the building and hopped into his car. At breakneck speed he flew down the freeway and made it to Laura's apartment in record time.

A sick feeling settled in the pit of his stomach as he pulled in behind two police cruisers. Their rotating lights lit up the tree-lined walkway. He climbed from his car, dashed into the building, and hurried up the stairs.

He burst through Laura's door and spotted her sitting on the sofa, an ice pack pressed to the side of her head. Erin sat with her while the officers, the same ones he'd encountered at the lab the previous night, muddled through the disorder and dusted for prints.

With determined strides, he stepped over a smashed lamp and crossed the room. He took one look at her ashen face and felt his blood run cold. She looked so fragile, so vulnerable. He wanted to take her into his arms and soothe away her troubles.

"God, Laura, are you okay?" He gestured for Erin to shove aside so he could sit next to her.

Laura forced a smile. "I'm fine."

"You're not fine." Mumbling curses under his breath, he placed his hand over the ice pack and held it in position for her. She looked exhausted and her body felt chilled. He glanced at Erin. "Would you mind grabbing a blanket?"

"Sure." Erin stood and disappeared down the hallway.

He turned his attention to Detective Doyle. "Who did this?"

"We're working on it," he assured him.

Jay gathered Laura into his arms and offered his warmth. Christ, he should have driven her home. If he'd been here for her, this never would have happened. Erin came back with a blanket. He took it from her and draped it over Laura's shoulders.

He felt his anger rising. "I assume it's connected to the lab break-in," he bit out.

The detective nodded. "Appears that way."

Laura's voice piped up. "He was after our files, but I came home before he found them."

She seemed so pleased by that fact. Jay carefully lifted the ice pack off her head and examined the bump. He winced. "The files don't matter, Laura. All that matters is that you're safe." His voice was tight with emotion. Oh God, what would he have done if something had happened to her? A sliver of unease made him flinch.

Her brow puckered in a frown. "Of course the files matter," she argued.

He placed the ice pack back over the lump. "I think you should see a doctor."

She waved a dismissive hand. "I'm fine," she insisted. "I don't need a doctor."

Jay glanced at the mess in her living room and drew a heavy breath. "You're coming to my place."

"No, I'm not," she said with certainty.

He wasn't about to take no for an answer. "Yes, you are, Laura."

"But—"

He interrupted her. "Don't argue with me. You're not staying here. Until they catch whoever did this you're not safe."

"I know it's not safe, Jay. Erin already said I could stay with her," she countered.

Jay twisted sideways and glared at Erin. He gave her a look that suggested it would be in her best interests to change Laura's mind.

Erin quickly caught on. She slapped her hand to her forehead. "Oh, I just remembered, you can't stay at my place after all. My spare room is being painted."

"There, that settles it. You're staying with me," Jay insisted.

She tensed against him. "Erin . . ." Laura's voice grated in warning.

Erin threw her hands up in the air and shrugged. "You know me and my forgetful memory."

Laura slumped back; her shoulders dropped. He felt her body relax against his and sensed her resolve was softening around the edges.

She gave a resigned groan. "Fine."

Jay rose from the couch and eased Laura to her feet. "Let me take you home and get you to bed."

As she stood, her curvy body collided with his. He splayed his hand on her back to anchor her to him. When her hips molded against his thighs, her breath seemed to hitch in her throat.

He watched the play of emotions cross her face and wondered what she was thinking. He decided not to press. There would be plenty of time for talking later when he had her snuggled in his bed. That thought brought a tingle to an area that needed to be ignored for the time being.

"I have to gather my things and have a quick shower."

He caught hold of her hand, grabbed her duffel bag from the floor, and escorted her down the hall. "Go shower." He held her bag out to her. "And then pack plenty, because until they find the guy who did this, you're staying with me."

He neglected to tell her that once he had her there, he didn't intend to let her go. Tonight he wanted to prove to Laura he wasn't just some playboy looking to get his hands on her sensuous body. She'd opened his eyes and his heart. He wanted her to be a part of his life.

Chapter 8

Night had closed around them by the time they stepped outside Laura's apartment and climbed into Jay's vehicle. Jay shot her a sidelong glance as he maneuvered his car into traffic. She'd changed into a pair of jeans that accentuated her curvy body and a pale yellow, short-sleeved blouse. Staring at the dark road ahead, she gently rubbed her fingers over the bump on her head. He touched her hand with his and gave a tender squeeze, bringing her attention around to him.

He arched one brow. "You sure you don't want to get that checked out?"

She dropped her hand in her lap and gave a quick shake of her head. "I'm fine, really," she assured him. "Besides, I don't feel like sitting at the hospital for hours just to have a doctor tell me I have a lump on my head. I already know that." She tossed him a genuine smile.

God, when she smiled at him like that his insides turned to mush. How in the hell would he ever be able to take her home, tuck her in his bed, and keep his hands to himself when all he could think about was kissing her, touching her, and finishing what they'd started in the director's bathroom?

He knew if he wanted her to see him as more than a sex-crazed playboy, more than "Wildman" Jay Cutler, he had to keep his hands to himself and figure out a game plan. Fast. He needed her to start thinking about him in terms of commitment, not just the hot roll in the hay for which he was known.

Christ, this was all so new to him. He'd never played for keeps before and he didn't want to screw it up. One thing was for certain. As long as she slept in his bed, he had to stay out of it. Hell, if he didn't, it would take more willpower than he could summon not to roll over and dust kisses over her entire body. To press his hips against her, draw her beaded nipples into his mouth for a thorough taste, spread her legs and sink his tongue into her damp heat. A plethora of fantasies rushed through his mind as he relished the provocative mental image.

Shit, his cock just skyrocketed to life.

He marshaled his thoughts and concentrated on the road ahead. Oh yeah, staying out of his bed was a definite must. No sense in testing temptation.

The sound of her stomach rumbling reached his ears. "Laura, you must be starving."

She nodded. "A little." Her stomach growled louder. She chuckled and said, "Okay, a lot."

"You never did eat that hot dog."

She glanced at him pointedly. "I got a little sidetracked, Jay. Had some . . . uh . . . research to do."

He returned with an apologetic glance. "Sorry about that."

"No, you're not." A bemused expression crossed her face.

A low chuckle rumbled in his throat. He threw his hands up in surrender. "Okay, I'm not, but I do take full responsibility."

She tipped her chin, her expression indignant. "I would think so," she added playfully.

"I know the perfect spot to take you. It's an authentic Italian restaurant where the recipes are handed down from generation to generation. You're going to love it." Suddenly his stomach joined in the chorus.

Laura chuckled, snuggled back in her seat, and said, "Sounds perfect."

Jay tapped the brakes, and then swung his car around in

the opposite direction. They both remained quiet, lost in their thoughts as he drove to the other side of town.

Less than a half an hour later, he pulled up along the curb in front of Isabella's. He killed the ignition and glanced around at his old stomping grounds.

Laura's face perked up. She squared her shoulders and sat up in her seat. "I've heard of this place, Jay. Don't we need a reservation?"

He grinned. "Nope. I have connections."

"You do? How?"

"I used to hang out here as a kid." He jerked his head forward. "I grew up just around the corner."

Green eyes opened wide, clearly intrigued. "Really? Are your parents still there?"

He gave a tight shake of his head. "No, my dad left when I was a kid and my mom . . . well . . . my mom and I never got along all that great. I guess I reminded her too much of my father." A pang of sadness fell over him like a heavy blanket. "She died a few years back."

She touched him with a comforting hand. "I'm sorry, Jay. I can't imagine what that must have been like. I got along well with my parents growing up. We still have dinner together every Sunday."

He smiled. Her concern filled him with warmth. He nodded toward the restaurant. "Tony and Isabella treated me like one of their own. I even put myself through college working in the kitchen." He opened his door. "Come on, let's go. I'm anxious for you to meet them."

He circled around the car and closed his large palm over hers. Rays from the streetlight hit the black pavement and spilled out in waves, touching the darkest corners of the streets. Laura shivered from the crispness in the cool evening air. Jay wrapped his arms around her, offering his warmth. Smiling up at him, she fell into step as he guided her inside.

As soon as he pulled open the door, the soft murmur of voices and mellow music rushed out to meet them. He breathed in the enticing aroma of fresh-baked bread and Italian sauces. The familiar sounds and smells filled him with contentment.

His gaze scanned the cozy restaurant and connected with Tony Moretti's.

Tony hurried across the room to greet him, his eyes wide with delight. His friendly robust voice and thick Italian accent wrapped around him and drew him in.

"Jay, my boy. Come, come in. Isabella will be so happy to see you. It has been too long." He threw his burly arms around Jay and squeezed. Dino, Jay's childhood best friend, came up beside Jay and the two exchanged a hug.

Tony turned to Dino. "Dino, call your mother."

A moment later, Isabella came bustling out of the kitchen. Jay's heart warmed at the sight of her. No matter how bad things had been at home, he'd always known he could count on Isabella. She'd treated him like one of her own, even scolded him and steered him in the right direction when he got into trouble. And he got into a lot of trouble.

Wiping her hands on her apron, she said, "Jay, come here." She hugged him and kissed both his cheeks. Wispy gray hair, always kept pulled back in a tight bun, tickled his skin. He inhaled her familiar comforting scent as she pulled him closer. Isabella stepped back, her brows furrowed. In the span of a moment she went from happy to mock angry. "What? You have no time for your family no more, now that you're a big fancy scientist in the city?"

"Sorry, Isabella. I've been working day and night. I promise to stop by more often. How is Grandmother?"

"Her ninety-eighth birthday is next month." She cocked a brow. "You'll come, yes?"

"Have I missed one yet?"

Smile restored, Isabella squeezed his cheeks, her face softened. "Ah, you are a good boy, Jay Cutler. You have a good heart." She turned to Tony and lifted her chin. "Did I not tell you he had a good heart?"

Tony sighed patiently. "Yeah, you did tell me, Issy. You told everybody. But we all knew he was a stand-up guy when he took my cousin's kid to the prom when her date stood her up."

Isabella's smile widened. "I knew you'd turn out different

from the others." Isabella turned to her husband Tony and threw her hands up in the air. "Did I not say he would turn out different from the others? That he wouldn't leave broken hearts all over the city like the rest of the rascals in his family? Jay is anything but a 'Cold-Hearted Cutler.'"

Jay swallowed the lump gathering in his throat. Up until recently, his track record certainly hadn't been so great. He was well on his way to following that fate. Jay snuck a peek at Laura. Thanks to her, he now knew there was more to him. His heart softened. He wanted to be a better man. For her. And for himself.

Tony gave a patient smile. "Yes, Isabella, you told us." He winked at Jay. "Many, many times."

Anchored to Jay's side, Laura stood there slack-jawed and soaked up the exchange between Jay and these warm, friendly people. She'd seen glimpses of his nurturing side many times before, but to see the shine in his eyes as he devoured the love around him made her heart ache with longing.

She took a moment to peruse the intimate restaurant. The atmosphere was easy, casual, and inviting, just like the owners. Balanced on top of red-and-white-checkered tablecloths she observed wax-coated Chianti bottle candle lamps. The walls were painted with vibrant hues, each color playing off the other.

Cathryn Fox

The sound of Jay's voice pulled her back. "I'd like you all to meet Laura. We work together at the lab." Jay turned to Laura and introduced Dino, Tony, and Isabella.

Planting her hands on her wide hips, Isabella focused her attention on Laura. Laura felt slightly uncomfortable as the woman's glance panned over her curvy figure, assessing her. Laura leaned into Jay, seeking his comfort.

"I like this girl, Jay. She doesn't look like a carrot stick. She has lovely round angles like a woman is supposed to have. She looks like she eats real food, not just lettuce."

As Laura smiled at Isabella's endorsement, she felt Jay's eyes trace the pattern of her shape. His pleasure resonated through her and made her pulse leap. It appeared to her that, although she didn't fit his usual descriptive requirements, Jay appreciated her curvy figure, too. Excitement coiled through her veins. Maybe he did have it bad for her.

Isabella turned back to Jay. "Is this one for keeps?"

Jay rolled his eyes and clutched Laura's hand. "Isabella, you ask me that every time."

She frowned and waved her hands wildly. "And I will keep asking until you give me the answer I'm looking for."

He squeezed Laura's hand. A gesture she was accustomed to, an indication to play along.

"Yes, Isabella, she's for keeps."

Laura's heart lodged in her throat and she worked furiously to swallow it down. If only he really *was* playing for keeps.

Features softening, Isabella clapped her hands together and threw her arms around Laura in a welcoming embrace. "I knew it, I knew it. Tony, come, we must celebrate." She flicked a glance at Dino. "Dino, seat them at the family table."

Dino motioned for them to follow. He fell into step beside Laura and whispered, "I hope you're not in a rush. Mother hasn't seen Jay in a couple of months and she'll want to go over every childhood story with him again. If you're really lucky, you'll escape before she brings out the photo album."

Laura smiled and felt an instant camaraderie with Dino. She gave a quick laugh as her second wind blew through her. "I'm in no rush at all."

Following Dino's lead, Laura and Jay moved toward a large round table at the back of the restaurant, just outside the kitchen doors.

Jay glanced at Laura and smiled. "Aren't they great?" She heard the pride in his voice.

"They're wonderful, Jay." It occurred to her that without these people, Jay never would have known love. "No wonder you hung out here." His smile widened, as though her approval of his extended family pleased him immensely.

With ten chairs around the table, Laura assumed they had one heck of a large clan. As she sat herself on a wooden chair padded with plush red velvet, the smells from the kitchen made her stomach rumble with hunger.

Tony came back with a bottle of Chardonnay and five glasses. As he poured the wine, Isabella smoothed back her silver hair, pulled off her apron, and sat beside Jay.

It was easy to tell how much she adored him. Laura knew the feelings were reciprocated.

Dino placed a loaf of fresh bread and whipped butter in the center of the table. The scent made her ravenous.

"Mmmm, that smells wonderful," Laura said.

Dino sat beside her. He leaned in and pitched his voice low. "Dig in. You may be here for a while."

As she shared a private chuckle with Dino, Laura felt Jay's eyes on her. She angled her head slightly and found him smiling. They exchanged a long lingering look. Warmth and familiarity rushed through her. God . . . when he looked at her like she was the most important person in the world, her knees turned to pudding.

An urgent flash of possessiveness rushed through her. Her heart reached out to him. Just below the surface, her blood simmered with need and desire and something else.

Something she didn't dare wish for. Something "Wildman" Jay Cutler had no intentions of handing her. Her stomach knotted like a pretzel. She never should have allowed herself to feel anything for him.

God, it frightened her how much she wanted him. She hungered to have him look at her with passion-imbued eyes, to touch her naked skin with his mouth, his tongue, and his fingers. To run her eager hands over his body in return and to finally finish what they had started in the director's bathroom.

Chest tight, she drew a breath, pushing down her wistful longing. Laura knew she needed to pull herself together. She sat back in her chair, sipped her wine, and nibbled on bread as Isabella carried the conversation, enlightening her to Jay's childhood antics.

Spending time with Jay outside the lab certainly played havoc on her emotions and pulled at her heartstrings. He was so easy, so comfortable. Being with him was as natural as breathing. Just watching him, his eyes bright with laughter as he refuted every wild story Isabella embellished, warmed her from the inside out. Reality disappeared when she was with him, making her forget they weren't really playing for keeps.

Laura marveled at the way his deep, sexy laugh curled around her and stirred her insides. She knew she was getting

Cathryn Fox

in deep. Way too deep. If she didn't soon erect a wall to protect her vulnerable heart, she'd need a compass to find her
way out.

Something told Laura that they'd barely scratched the
surface on Isabella's stories when a young, handsome dark-
skinned man stuck his head out from the kitchen. "Isabella, you're needed."

"Yes, Carlos, I'll be right there." Exasperated, she threw
her hands up in the air. "What would they do without
me?"

"Well, if you would share your secret family recipes
with Carlos, he could make the sauces for you," Tony said.

She wagged a warning finger at Tony, then turned her
attention to Jay. Before rising, Isabella captured Jay's face
in her palms. "Ah, Jay, you have grown into such a handsome, respectable man. People still come into the restaurant looking for you. Looking for your specialty."

He looked down shyly and reached for his glass. He
drained his wine as a blush rose up his neck.

Laura's heart turned over in her chest. She couldn't believe the adorable sight before her. Jay Cutler blushing?
Well, hell, now she'd seen it all.

Laura took a small sip of her wine. "What specialty?"
she asked, not really sure she wanted to hear the answer,
especially after experiencing his personal brand of *specialty*.

148

Isabella kissed her fingertips and threw her hands in the air. "Jay makes one primo linguine noodle." Her chest puffed up proudly. "I taught him everything."

"But you still haven't taught me how to make the sauce that goes with it," he teased.

She made a face and wagged her finger at Jay. "Why, you . . ." Isabella rose and retied her apron.

Laura arched a brow. "Really? A primo linguine noodle?" Impressive. Especially for someone who could screw up a box of macaroni and cheese. "Now, that I'd like to see."

"Then you must," Isabella said.

Tony set his wineglass down on the table. "Issy, leave the boy alone."

Ignoring Tony, Isabella stood. "Come, Jay. Show Laura what you can do." Isabella's grin widened. The affection the older woman felt for Jay radiated off her and warmed everyone at the table.

Jay caught Laura's glance. When a hesitant frown crossed his face, Laura reached out and touched him. "I would love to watch you make linguine, Jay," she reassured. "In fact, I'd love for you to teach me."

His eyes met hers and held. Something intimate, tender passed between them and made her breath catch. Her pulse kicked into high gear. For a fleeting second he gazed at her like he really was playing for keeps.

Cathryn Fox

Could it be possible?

Did she dare hope?

"That settles it, then. Come, both of you."

Laura followed Isabella into the kitchen. The fresh scent of spices assailed her senses. She'd never been privy to the inner workings of a restaurant kitchen before. She took a moment to catalogue her surroundings. Taking stock, she watched a few male cooks mill around. The men shot her a smile as they prepared scrumptious platters of pasta. One man slid what appeared to be a double cheese, meat lover's pizza, or, as Laura preferred to call it, the coronary, in a brick oven, then resumed his position at a gas stove where hearty sauces thickened and boiled on the burners. His head bounced in time to the beat of a song drifting in from a nearby speaker. It was all so wonderful and quaint.

From across the room she heard Carlos call out. "J-man, it's good to see you." He scrubbed his hand over his neatly trimmed goatee as his dark gaze went to Jay, then Laura. With a long, languorous glance, he skimmed Laura's curves. His strides were determined, sensuous as he strode across the kitchen and stepped into her personal space. In a slick, sexy Italian accent he said to Jay, "And who is this gorgeous lady you have brought for me?"

Laura glanced at his eagle tattoo, then crimped her neck to look in his eyes. Carlos inclined his head and met her gaze straight on. Thick black hair spilled forward over rich, seductive eyes. Testosterone oozed from his pores. Lord, the man had bad boy written all over him.

"Hello there," he said. His deep masculine voice could curl toes.

In a protective manner, Jay tucked Laura under his arm and grinned. "Stay away from this guy, Laura," he warned. Even though humor edged his voice, she sensed an underlying possessiveness in his tone. "He'll get you into trouble every time." Jay dipped his head and whispered into her hair, "I know firsthand." His sweet wine-scented breath tickled her neck and seeped into her blood, arousing all her senses, filling her with longing.

Laura shook her arousal-fogged brain and extended her arm. "Nice to meet you, Carlos." For a moment she wondered if he was Isabella's son.

As though reading her thoughts, Jay piped in, "Carlos lived two houses down from me." He gestured with a nod. "This is the guy who was responsible for all the trouble and fights Dino and I got into as teens until Isabella took him under her wing and straightened him out."

It amazed Laura how these people opened their home and hearts to others. No wonder they had so many chairs around the huge table.

"Isabella has filled me in on some of Jay's antics, but it sounds like you have a few stories of your own. I'd love to hear them," she prompted with a smile.

A wicked grin curled his lips. Carlos opened his mouth to speak.

Jay cut him off with a glare. "Forget it, Carlos," he rushed out, sparing Laura the details.

Goading Jay on, Carlos stepped closer and took her hand in his. Using the pad of his thumb, he caressed her skin and then with a quick tug pulled her away from Jay. "Forget J-man's specialty, Laura, come sample mine instead," he teased. His sexy voice was as smooth as spun silk.

Laura took her hand back, angled her chin, and arched a brow. "Yes, Jay. I can see how Carlos could have gotten you into trouble a time or two," she said, joining in the teasing. She glanced at Jay. "I'm sure you and Dino were simply innocent bystanders," she added, humoring him.

"Naturally," he confirmed. Jay crooked his finger for her to come back, his eyes full of teasing warmth. Without taking his gaze off Laura, he said, "How many times have I told you, Carlos? Once a woman has sampled fine dining, she'll never go back to fast food."

Carlos roared with laughter. Eyes glistening from their easy banter, Carlos brushed his thumb and forefinger over his mustache and razzed Jay. He gifted Laura with a sexy wink. "And I've told you, J-man. Once a woman has sampled a zesty Italian menu"—he paused to tap his chest—"nothing else will ever satisfy her hunger."

This time Jay roared with laughter.

They held her spellbound as they good-naturedly ribbed one another. Jay slipped his arm around her waist, snatching her back. She stepped into his embrace and snuggled into the circle of his arms. That small affectionate gesture seemed to please him.

Jay chuckled as Isabella swatted Carlos on the backside, shooing him to the other side of the kitchen. "You . . ." she said. "You got too many ladies to take care of already. Come on, Laura, I've cleared a spot on the counter for you and Jay."

Jay had never found pasta-making an erotic experience before. Then again, he'd never made linguine with a sexy scientist before. Laura was as brilliant in the lab as she was inept in the kitchen. Twenty minutes into the process, she had more flour on her face, her clothes, and in her hair than they had on the counter. But by God, he had to admit, she looked appealing as hell in such a disheveled state.

Standing behind her, Jay watched as she awkwardly squeezed the dough between her fingers like she had a personal vendetta against it. He shook his head and chuckled.

"Laura, you really suck at this."

She tipped her head back. Her lips puckered. Taking great offense to his words, she cocked her chin indignantly and said, "Excuse me. Did you just say I suck?"

153

Jay grinned, brushed her long chestnut locks from her face, and tucked them behind her ear. "Yes, I believe that's the technical term."

She pinched some flour between her fingers and sprinkled it on him. "Hey, play nice."

He winked at her. "I always play nice."

The doubtful expression on her face told him she knew otherwise.

He waved his hand toward the deformed blob on the counter. "What the hell did that dough ever do to you?"

Laura laughed and slanted her head. "You mean it's not supposed to look all lumpy like this?" Her low, throaty chuckle played down his spine and filled him with warmth.

He stepped closer and stood behind her. "I'm afraid not. It's all in the kneading. Watch me." Slipping his hands around her waist, enclosing her in the circle of his arms, he interlaced his fingers through hers and began kneading the dough. With his chest nestled against her back, her cushiony bottom pressed against his groin. The position brought back heated memories of their earlier afternoon activities. He quickly censored his thoughts and curbed his desires. Good Lord, he wasn't supposed to be thinking about such things when he was trying to prove he was more than just a playboy.

He tried to keep his voice level. "Nice and slow, using the ball of your hand. Keep kneading it until the flour is mixed and the texture is smooth." As he leaned over her, the familiar scent of her freshly shampooed hair assailed his senses, intoxicating him. He inhaled and refrained from brushing his lips along her cheekbone.

She whacked his hands away, reminding him of her stubborn streak and how she always faced a challenge straight on. Damn, he loved that about her.

"Okay, I get it. Let me try."

Jay stepped back and watched her. It was easy to tell she was enjoying herself. With single-minded determination, her sole focus was to master pasta-making. As she took another stab at the dough, his lips twitched with amusement.

She tossed the words over her shoulder. "I think I got it now, Jay." With innocent sensuality she rocked back and forth on her heels, rolling the dough on the counter.

From the other side of the kitchen Carlos called out to him. "Hey J-man, this song is for you." Carlos cranked up the radio. The song "Play That Funky Music" echoed through the kitchen.

Laura began to sing and dance along. Her long hair tumbled over her shoulders as her head bounced to the music.

Despite Jay's best attempt to direct his gaze away from her perfectly sculpted backside, he couldn't. Instead, he stood there, transfixed, taking great pleasure in the way Laura swayed her curvy hips to the beat.

Humming to the tune, she made small sensuous moves, the same ones she'd made when she'd danced for him at her apartment after he'd won the coin toss. His gaze raked over her. No matter how hard he tried, he couldn't dispel the image of the way she'd seductively stripped off her lacy lingerie, the way the candlelight glistened on her naked flesh, or the way she responded to his touch. His body tightened with the memory.

The sound of her melodic voice and the sight of her tight jeans hugging the swell of her ass as she undulated to the beat elevated his pulse. His blood pressure soared. His resolve dissolved like sugar in water.

A sudden burst of passion roared through him like a freight train as he watched her hypnotic movements. Blood rushed to his cock, taking his common sense with it. Lust settled deep in his groin. His throat clenched. Jesus Christ, it was impossible to resist her.

In that instant, all he could think about was sliding his cock into her slick heat. A growl of sexual frustration climbed up his throat. His cock strained to break free from its zippered cage. Fuck. He lived in a constant state of arousal around her.

He sucked in a tight breath and took another step back, keeping his distance before he did something he'd regret. Like spinning her around and pressing his hungry mouth over hers and devouring her until they were both delirious with the need to drop to the floor and ravage one another. He ached for her to climb over him, to ride him furiously, until her silken sex tightened and contracted around his cock and her hot creamy essence flowed over his shaft.

A violent shudder overtook him.

"Ta-da!" she said, spinning around. She offered him a smile that touched his heart. Warm familiarity curled around him. "I did . . ." When her gaze collided with his, her words died away. Surprise registered on her face as she instantly became aware of the passion rising in him.

God, she looked so beautiful. His nostrils flared. Swallowing, he called on every ounce of strength and fought the urge to close the gap between them.

"I . . . uh . . . I think I got it," she whispered with effort. Her pink tongue snaked out to wet her lips.

He felt his body moisten from fever. Closing his eyes in distress, he worked to fight his traitorous libido. He took another small step back.

"Jay . . ." Her soft tone gained his full attention. He opened his eyes and met her glance. Color bloomed high on her cheeks.

The sexy lilt of her voice and the way his name rolled off her tongue penetrated his resolve and propelled him forward. The overwhelming need to touch her and to taste the sweetness of her mouth overshadowed rational thought.

No longer able to ignore his cravings, he drew a shaky breath, reversed his backward direction, and moved into her space. One kiss. God, his mouth begged for just one small kiss.

Green eyes widened as he crowded her. So much for keeping his physical distance. He was so fucking weak when it came to her.

Jay swallowed and worked to speak. "You have flour on your face." His voice dropped an octave.

With slow movements, he reached out and brushed the white powder from her cheek. She shivered under his touch. Unexpectedly, her hand closed over his. She nestled against him, their eyes locked. His breath hitched when she touched him in a way no other woman had ever touched him before. Emotionally, not physically. Was it possible she saw him as something more than "Wildman" Jay Cutler?

Hope filled him.

He cleared his throat. A rush of tenderness passed through him as she tightened her fingers over his. Working to lighten the mood before all control was obliterated and he gave in to his urges, he glanced at the smooth ball of dough and pitched his voice low.

"You're a fast learner, Laura. Maybe next time you can share your specialty with me."

Her eyes brimmed with desire. "The only thing I can make is ice cubes." Her warm breath tickled his flesh, fragmenting his thoughts.

He forced a quick laugh as his mind conjured up the wonderful things they could do with said ice cubes.

He tried not to concentrate on the sensations as her hips joined with his. He really did. But when she rose up on her tippy toes, the feel of her warm sex pressed against his drew his attention. She let out a little breath. It was hot on his neck. "You have flour on your cheeks, Jay." With the backs of her fingers she wiped it away.

"And you have flour everywhere, sweetheart," he countered, his tone full of want.

Her hair spilled from its moorings and tumbled over her shoulders as she glanced down at her blouse. "So I see." When she tipped her chin to meet his eyes, he brushed his thumb over her lips. He was ready to explode just from caressing her lush mouth.

"Even in your hair," he added, curling her tips around his finger. Desire crept into his voice, despite his efforts to bank it.

Sexual energy jetted between them. His cock jerked in anticipation.

Her slender arms circled his neck. She glanced around, taking note of the cooks milling about, tending to their own business, and then, unexpectedly, she parted her plump lips and drew his finger into her mouth.

Holy shit!

A growl rose from the depths of his throat. His mind shut down. Her boldness shocked the hell out of him.

She drew him in deep and sucked long and hard. Her eyes clouded with emotions and Jay knew the situation was escalating beyond his power to stop it.

Everything in him reached out to her.

Momentarily forgetting where they were, he gathered her into his embrace. Their bodies melded as he dipped his head and skated his tongue over the seam of her lips. She shivered under his touch. He could feel her hard nipples press insistently against his chest. She parted her mouth in invitation. No longer able to smother his desires, Jay drew her in for a soul-searching kiss. A soft moan of surrender rumbled in his throat as he ran his fingers over the contours of her body.

He savored the satiny warmth of her mouth as his lips closed over hers. He insinuated his tongue in between her petaled softness, seeking his mate. The sweet invasion made his knees weak. The heat from her mouth boiled his blood to dangerous levels. Her erotic whimper urged him on. He deepened the kiss and growled as he gave in to his desires.

Jay ran his hands down to the small of her back and slipped his fingers under her blouse. He drew lazy circles on her flesh as he found solace in their embrace. She let out a broken gasp as they remained pressed up against each other for the longest moment.

"Hey, J-man," Carlos called out.

Laura broke the kiss. Her eyes opened wide. She stepped back, freeing herself from the circle of his arms, breaking the spellbinding moment. He immediately missed her touch. In a knee-jerk reaction, he cupped her elbow and pulled her back.

"Laura . . ." he whispered.

"Get a room," Carlos teased.

Reality crashed down on him like a storm at the sound of Carlos's voice.

Well, fuck.

He let her arm go.

Nice move, dumb ass! he thought. Way to prove you're not a playboy.

To her. And to himself.

Jay cursed himself for giving in to his impulses. Laura deserved to be treated better.

Troubled by his actions, he glanced at her apologetically. Emotions churned in the turbulent depths of her eyes, making him twice as determined to prove himself worthy of her.

Cathryn Fox

Clenching his jaw, Jay took a step back, distancing himself. "Why don't we grab a slice?" He nodded at the pizza coming out of the brick oven. "We'll let Carlos finish up here and then pack the linguine to go."

Chapter 9

Laura folded her hands on her lap and let her gaze pan across Jay's strong profile as he negotiated his car through traffic. His masculine scent saturated the tight confines of the vehicle and curled around her. Inhaling, she studied his handsome face for a long, thoughtful moment.

"Hey, J-man," she said softly.

He slanted his head and smirked. "Yeah?"

"Thank you for tonight."

His smile warmed her heart.

"Thank *you*," he said. "It was fun."

"I really enjoyed meeting your family."

"They enjoyed meeting you, too."

She reached out and touched his hand. "I always have fun when I'm with you."

He arched a brow and squeezed her fingers. "Oh yeah? Even when I bowled you over at the ball game?"

Laura chuckled. "Well, I guess there are a few exceptions."

She tapped the brown paper bag that Isabella had generously filled with containers of fresh pasta and sauce. "Thanks for teaching me how to make pasta. I'll have to wait until tomorrow to eat it, though." She rubbed her stomach. "I'm full from the pizza." God, how she loved sitting there chatting with him. Their easy conversations always tugged at her insides.

Darkness blanketed the parking lot as he pulled his car into his assigned space. As she played over the events of the evening, her thoughts returned to Isabella.

She twisted sideways in her seat to face Jay. "Jay, what did Isabella mean when she said you weren't just another 'Cold-Hearted Cutler'?"

He got quiet for a moment, and then frowned in concentration. "My father and the rest of the men in the Cutler family had never had a lasting relationship. They were all playboys and were emotionally unavailable. After my father left us, my mother nicknamed them all 'Cold-Hearted Cutlers.'" He glanced at her as though gauging her reaction.

She nodded, prodding him on. He drew a breath and continued. "And I was always told I wouldn't amount to anything different."

Her heart went out to him. She lowered her voice, appreciating his honesty. She wanted to be honest with him, too. She crinkled her nose and said in the nicest possible way, "Your track record hasn't been great so far."

Emotions passed over his eyes. A muscle in his jaw clenched. "I know."

"It sounds like Isabella and Tony always had faith in you. Believed you'd be different."

He rolled his shoulders. "They did, but when you hear something often enough, that you'd never turn out any different than your father, you begin to live up to those expectations."

She nodded in understanding. "So what would it take for you to prove to yourself that you're not just another 'Cold-Hearted Cutler'?"

His head came up slowly. "The right woman," he replied, his dark eyes brimming with emotion.

When he glanced in her eyes, her breath stalled. He gave her a long, lingering look. It was the same look he'd given her at the restaurant. The one that made her feel like the most important woman in the world. The one that made her wonder if he really was interested in playing for keeps.

Her heart did a somersault.

When he'd told Isabella that Laura was for keeps, was he just appeasing her, like Laura had thought, or was it possible that *Laura* was the right woman?

God, did she dare hope?

Suddenly Jay glanced over her shoulder. She turned her head. "What is it?"

"I don't know. I thought I saw something rush by. After the break-in at the lab and your apartment I don't want to take any chances. I want to get you inside and keep you safe."

Laura's heart picked up tempo. She squinted her eyes and peered into the darkness. "I don't see anything, Jay." It occurred to her that maybe he was just trying to shift the focus away from him. Maybe he didn't want to pursue the conversation or talk about emotional commitment.

"Come on, let's get inside," Jay said.

Jay gathered the bags of food while Laura fished her hand around the back seat until she found her duffel bag.

Jay circled the car to meet her. No sooner had they taken a step toward the building than two masked men came out of the shadows.

"Shit," Jay cursed, grabbing Laura to position her behind him. "Get back in the car and lock the doors," he said between gritted teeth. He widened his stance, preparing for battle.

"Not so fast," one of the hooded men blurted, and

pulled something out from behind his back. Light from the apartment building glistened on the blade of the knife the man wielded.

"Give me your bag."

Confused, Laura jerked her head up. They wanted the linguine?

Standing behind Jay, Laura peered around his shoulder and nudged his back. "Give him the bag, Jay."

The masked man's quick, jerky movements as his gaze flitted around the parking lot alerted Laura to his discomfort.

"Not that one," he said, shaking his head in frustration.

Geez. Well, it wasn't like he'd specified.

Impatience mingled with nervousness and laced the man's voice. Laura sensed he wasn't really out to hurt them, sensed he didn't want any more trouble than she did.

He gestured to her duffel bag. "That bag."

Her clothes? They wanted her clothes?

Great, they were being accosted by cross-dressing thugs.

Charming.

The other man remained silent as he carefully circled them and stalked up behind Laura. There was something hauntingly familiar about the way he moved.

Laura snaked her arms around Jay's waist. He closed his

hands over hers and held her tight. Even though they were being attacked by two hooded men, she felt absurdly safe in his arms.

"You know what we're after," the masked man growled.

Understanding dawned on Laura. Clearly they were idiots if they thought her files were in her duffel bag. But hell, who was she to argue? They were the ones with the weapon.

"Hand him the bag," the knife-wielding man said, nudging his chin toward the guy closing in on her. "And no one gets hurt."

Shoot, why in the hell hadn't she stuck with those self-defense lessons? She really didn't want some thugs from Ad-Tech running off with her delicates.

In a motion so fast it took the two masked men off guard, Laura mustered all her strength and jabbed her elbow into the creep's stomach as he stepped into her personal space.

He let out a whoosh of air.

Jesus Christ! She immediately recognized that ungodly scent. Come to think of it, an open coffin might even smell better.

Distracted, the knife-wielding man turned his attention to Laura. A string of profanity spewed from his mouth. With his attention directed on her, Jay went for the guy's blade. He kicked it out of his hand and with one powerful punch knocked the guy to the ground.

Impressive!

Before Jay had a chance to come to her rescue, Laura slammed her foot down on Max's instep, lifted her arm to take a crack at his nose, and then finished him off with a pounding to the groin. Not that she'd ever wanted to go anywhere near Max's groin.

Thank you, Gracie Hart!

Max cursed under his breath as he cupped his balls in agony. He staggered to his feet, grabbed her duffel bag, and disappeared into the darkness.

Damn, all that work and Crouton Boy made off with her delicates anyway. She shook her head. At least now she understood why Max had been so persistent, trying to charm his way into her apartment. He wasn't after her, he was after her formula.

Laura turned her attention to Jay and watched him pull his cell phone out of his pocket as the masked man rolled out of his reach, stumbled to his feet, and ran in the same direction as Max.

Breathless, Jay met her gaze. His eyes were full of tender concern. "Are you okay?"

She nodded. "You?"

"Yeah. Where the hell did you learn that?"

Laura drew in air and shook the sting from her hand. "Last weekend I had a date with Ben and Jerry and *Miss Congeniality 2: Armed and Fabulous.*"

He frowned in confusion. "Do you want to try that again? In English this time."

"Ben and Jerry's is a brand of ice cream and *Miss Congeniality 2* is a movie with Sandra Bullock." She mimicked her earlier actions. "I put Gracie Hart's SING technique—solar plexus, instep, nose, and groin—to use."

He shook his head in amazement. "I never knew you were a woman of so many talents. Remind me never to piss you off."

Jay pulled a card out of his back pocket. "We need to call the detective." He punched the number into his cell phone.

"Good, because I know who is responsible."

Jay's fingers stopped. "You do?"

"Yeah. Max."

His head jerked back. His brow puckered. "Max? How do you know it was Max?"

"By his breath. I can identify him."

He gave her a look that suggested she'd lost more than her delicates.

"I'm not crazy, Jay."

"We didn't see their faces, Laura. We can't identify them." He cocked a brow and grinned. "Unless, of course, they put him in a breath smelling lineup?"

"Good idea." She waved her hands impatiently. "Give me the phone."

Jay handed it to her.

It rang twice before she heard Detective Doyle's booming voice on the other end.

Still trying to regulate her breathing, Laura quickly relayed the details to the detective.

Doyle got quiet for a moment. Laura assumed he had to swallow a bite of donut before he could speak. Finally, he cleared his throat and spoke. "I'll pay him a visit, but I'll need more proof than bad breath, Laura."

Angered, she opened her mouth to argue, but he cut her off.

"Don't worry, all is not lost. We found a print at your apartment and they're running it."

They spoke for a few more minutes and then she handed the phone back to Jay. "He wants to talk to you."

Jay exchanged a few words, assured the detective they were okay, and promised to come in first thing in the morning to fill out a report.

Jay slid the phone back into his pocket and glanced at her. "He told us to sit tight and stay inside. Tomorrow we'll give a statement." He grabbed her hand. "Come on, let's go before they realize they made off with your clothes. Although something tells me they won't be back." He grinned. "Not after you going all Jackie Chan on them. That guy's going to be nursing his balls for a while."

*   *   *

Laura kicked off her shoes in Jay's front foyer and perused her surroundings. His place wasn't at all what she had expected. He might live a sexy playboy lifestyle, but his apartment looked nothing like a Don Juan bachelor pad. Of course, it didn't really surprise her. Underneath that playboy façade existed a caring, nurturing man. Maybe even a nerdy scientist at heart.

His spacious front entrance opened into a very masculine, yet comfortable living area. Off that room, she spotted a bright yellow kitchen with a small dinette table tucked in the corner.

"I'll take your things to the bedroom."

The sound of his deep sleepy voice pulled at her. God, she couldn't believe how much she wanted him. How much she wanted him to want her the same way.

She fell into step behind him and admired his broad, muscular back as she followed him down the hall. He pushed open the door and gestured for her to enter.

One bed, of gigantic proportions, filled the room. Her gaze darted to his headboard, searching for notches. She wondered how many women had writhed beneath Jay on that slate-blue duvet. She squeezed her lids tight, shutting out that unwelcome thought as her galloping heart took her on a turbulent emotional journey.

When she opened her eyes, realization hit full force. It occurred to her she hadn't seen Jay with a woman in months. And come to think of it, the phone hadn't been ringing off the hook at the lab. Was it because they'd been working so hard on the project, or was it because he'd lost his taste for carrot sticks?

Suddenly overcome by exhaustion, Laura yawned and rolled one shoulder. She winced as her muscles strained. She must have pulled something when she took Max out.

Jay's expression turned serious. Reaching out, he palmed her arm and began a slow massage. She started at his touch. His big warm hand swallowed up her entire shoulder. They were so strong and powerful, yet touched her with such tenderness.

As she looked into his gentle eyes, her mind raced. She thought about all the years they'd worked together and assignments they'd completed. She thought about all the ball games they'd played together, the bonding sessions they'd attended, and all the laughs they'd shared. She thought about their intimate night at her place and their afternoon in the director's bathroom. She thought about meeting his family at the restaurant and pasta-making in the kitchen.

Her heart tightened in her chest. God, they were so good together.

She replayed the passionate kiss he'd given her only hours earlier. If the enhancer had still been ruling his body, surely his kiss wouldn't have been so tender, so emotional.

She thought about the way Jay made her feel. He made

her see herself as something other than a nerdy scientist. For the first time she believed her curvaceous body was beautiful, and that her intelligence was something to be proud of.

She paused to consider things.

Maybe now it was her turn to make Jay see himself as something other than a playboy. To show him he was nothing like the men in his family. Jay was gentle and caring and if there was one thing she knew for certain, he was capable of love.

Laura drew a fueling breath. Tonight, she was going to do something she'd never done before. She was going to step out of her comfort zone and take a big risk.

She was going to show Jay he wasn't another "Cold-Hearted Cutler." And most importantly, she was going to show him she was the *right woman*, dammit.

And how was she going to do that? By seducing Jay's body and his heart and finishing what they started. She was going to make sweet love to him all night long and reveal she was interested in playing for keeps. And during their lovemaking she planned on touching him on a deeper level, to show him he had the ability to feel emotions.

"You're so stiff."

Jay's voice pulled her thoughts to the present.

He stepped closer, his warm masculine scent curling around her. Swallowing hard, she concentrated on the tiny points of pleasure as her senses exploded. She resisted the urge to glance downward, to see if he was *stiff* too.

She fought to find her voice. "Probably from when I slammed my elbow into Max."

"You've really taken a beating today, haven't you?"

"I've had better days," she agreed. "At least you weren't responsible for all of my injuries," she teased.

He smiled. "How about a long soak in the tub? That should help ease the ache."

Laura shivered as her mind conjured up other ways Jay could help ease her aches. Ways like he had earlier that afternoon.

He didn't wait for her to answer. "Come on." Capturing her hand in his, he led her across the hall. "I'll run it for you."

Heat and strength radiated from him and warmed her all over as he guided her to the bathroom. She sat on the edge of his gray porcelain tub and watched him adjust the water temperature. As her heart turned over in her chest, she wondered exactly when it was that she'd fallen in love with him.

"That should do it." He tilted his head. "I'll grab you one of my T-shirts to wear. I'll be back in a minute."

Her body tingled in anticipation as she counted the seconds.

Before he left her alone to bathe in private, he lit a candle

Cathryn Fox

and dimmed the lights. The perfect atmosphere for a seduction, she mused.

Minutes later she found herself stretched out in his bathtub. The candle flickering on the counter provided soft lighting while the warm, heated water soothed her tired, aching muscles. She washed her body, then dropped the scented bar of soap, letting it fall between her thighs.

A moment later a knock sounded on the door. "Come in," she said, wondering why he was knocking. It wasn't like he bothered knocking earlier today when he caught her in her underwear in the director's bathroom.

"Are you decent?" he asked.

That depended on what he considered decent. Her thoughts certainly weren't. "I'm naked."

His chuckle reverberated through the door. "If I see anything I've never seen before, I'll shoot it."

Always the smart-ass. Before she had time to answer, the door inched open.

He pitched his voice low. "I just thought you'd like a cup of tea. I know how you like to have a cup before bed."

"Oh yeah?" She raised a curious brow. "How do you know that?"

He shrugged. "You always have a cup at the lab when we work late."

She gazed at his handsome face shimmering in the golden candlelight. "Thanks." Her heart reached out to him.

"You're welcome." He held the cup out for her and perched on the side of the tub.

God, she couldn't believe how jittery, how vulnerable she suddenly felt. Then again, it wasn't every day she stepped out of her comfort level and offered herself completely to Jay, body and heart. And she was about to find out, once and for all, whether the enhancer had been ruling his actions or if he really had it bad for her.

She drew a fortifying breath, sat up, and exposed her soapy breasts as she accepted the hot tea. She took a small sip. "Mmmm. It's good," she whispered. Seemingly pleased, the corners of his mouth lifted in a half smile.

He dipped one hand in the water and ran his warm, wet fingers along the back of her neck. She loved how he touched her in such a familiar way. Her body shuddered at the onslaught of pleasure.

Working on her seduction skills, she leaned forward and blew into her mug. Long wisps of wet hair spilled forward and brushed across her nipples. The sensation hardened her pale buds.

She tilted her head back and watched Jay, gauging his reaction.

The cords on his throat worked as his gaze dropped from her mouth to her breasts. By small degrees she noted the change in his posture. He compressed his lips as he drove his fingers through his tousled hair.

Was that desire she spotted in his baby blues before he averted his gaze? A thrill rushed through her.

Instantaneously, her bliss disappeared when he leapt from the side of the tub. Conflicting emotions churned in his eyes. The change in his mood occurred so swiftly it caught her off guard.

"You should get some sleep. It's late, and you've been through a lot tonight." His voice sounded tight. "And we have a lot of work to do tomorrow." He pulled his robe from the hook beside the vanity and draped it across the sink before he left. "I laid a T-shirt out for you on the bed." The sound of the door clicking shut behind him left her chilled.

At that precise moment she knew it for certain; her worst fears were confirmed. Not only was Jay not interested in playing for keeps, he didn't even have it bad for her.

The lingering effects of the enhancer had been ruling his actions.

Laura swallowed the lump clogging her throat. She was never going to walk out of this apartment with her heart intact.

Feeling very weary, she climbed from the tub, quickly towel-dried herself, and hurried back to his room. After slipping into one of his long T-shirts, she turned the light off, climbed into his bed, and drew the covers up to her neck.

Burying her face into the pillowcase, she inhaled. His masculine scent permeated the sheets.

Slivers of silvery light from the full moon high overhead drifted in through the parted curtains and bathed the bed in a warm sensual glow, setting the perfect mood for lovers. Lovers! Cripes, how could she have ever let herself believe they were lovers? That there was more between them? This was all just a goddamn experiment. Now she really wished she had stayed in those self-defense classes, so she could kick her own ass!

"How are you feeling? Do you need anything?"

His soft whisper startled her. Her gaze darted to the door. He stood there, leaning against the doorjamb, his hands deep in the pockets of his jeans, looking so damn handsome.

She worked to sound casual as her heart beat in a mad cadence. "No. I'm fine."

"How about the bump on your head? Does it still hurt?"

She brushed her fingertips over the bump. "The swelling has gone down." Swelling. Oh God, her mind conjured up the wicked ways Jay had taken down her swelling earlier that day.

Jay crossed the room. The mattress dipped as he sat on the edge of the bed. She propped her head on her palm, her hair falling across her face.

He reached out and tucked the wayward strands behind her ear. "I'm glad it wasn't worse."

A shiver tingled all the way to her toes. "I consider it a small price to pay for saving the files. I don't want anyone perfecting the libido suppressant before us."

His eyes opened wide and he threw his hands in the air. "Laura, in all the commotion I forgot to tell you. The suppressant worked on Clyde."

She jolted upright. "You're kidding." When he shook his head, she rushed on. "That's fantastic. Surely the board will approve our grant based on those results."

He shrugged. "Not sure. The side effects may be different on humans. I think we should test it on ourselves once more just to be certain."

She nibbled on her lower lip and dropped her head back onto his pillow. "I guess you're right. We'll want to have all bases covered and all questions answered before we present our findings." She grew quiet, thoughtful for a moment. They hadn't come this far for her to back down now. The success of the project was too important to too many people for her to let her emotions get in the way.

"I'll inject you at the end of the day tomorrow."

He tucked the blankets around her, and dropped the sweetest, softest kiss on her forehead. A kiss filled with so much tenderness and emotion it amazed her. Whoa. What the hell was that? A man who wasn't interested in playing for keeps didn't kiss like that.

He slipped from the bed and in three long strides crossed

the room. He turned back to face her. "There's no need for you to go into the lab in the morning. We're going to work from home tomorrow. I'm only going to go in long enough to get the suppressant, then I'll come back and we'll get started right away at testing the stability and the side effects."

He stood in the doorway, his large body practically blocking all the light spilling in from the hall.

"Can you administer it to yourself?"

He shook his head. "Since Erin already knows what we're up to, I'll have her do it for me."

Oh God, her heart stopped. She sucked in a quick breath, shocking it back to life. She'd better get hold of Erin before she did something stupid.

Like switch the vials.

Unable to get comfortable on the sofa, Jay fitfully tossed and turned until the wee hours of the morning. The beautiful vision of Laura lying in his tub rushed through his mind like a hurricane. His cock stirred to life just thinking about it. And knowing she was only seconds from his touch continued to add fuel to the fire. He resisted the urge to reach into his boxers to take care of that huge problem.

By four-thirty he'd given up on trying to sleep. Tossing the thin sheet aside, he climbed from the sofa, stretched out his tired limbs, and walked quietly down the hall.

He peeked into his bedroom and watched Laura sleep. She looked so peaceful, angelic. Sometime throughout the night she'd kicked off her blankets. They lay in a rumpled pool at the foot of the bed. His long T-shirt tangled around her thighs while her silky legs stretched across the mattress. He walked over to the bed, grabbed the blankets, and covered her.

He noticed the bedside alarm was set for five. An hour before she normally woke up. Why would she do that? She had no reason to get up that early. They'd already agreed that they would work from home today. Bending down, he turned the alarm off, allowing her to rest as long as her exhausted mind and body needed to.

She mumbled something in her sleep and rolled onto her side. He fought down the urge to crawl in next to her. Just to hold her in his arms. But he didn't want to wake her up. She needed to sleep. Especially for what he had planned for them tonight.

Last night, he'd shown her another side of him. Shown her there was more to him than just a sex-crazed playboy. That he could be around her without ravishing her gorgeous body. And at the restaurant he'd shown her how good they could be together outside the lab.

Tonight, however . . . tonight was a different story. He wanted to show her how good they could be between the sheets. His sheets. It was time to finish what they'd started.

He wanted to take his time and make slow, passionate love to her, until she gave herself over to him.

Suddenly it dawned on him that they were to test the stability of the libido suppressant.

He frowned. Damn.

That was really going to put a crimp in his plans.

Chapter *10*

Laura's exhausted body fought against the sound of chirping birds intruding on her well-deserved slumber. Her eyes fluttered open, and then slid shut against the bright sunshine seeping through the paneled curtains. She shifted and snuggled into the warm sheets.

Her tender muscles ached, bringing back memories of every erotic activity she'd engaged in with Jay.

The birds continued chirping, pulling her awake. She stretched, feeling more refreshed than she had in ages. She opened her eyes and glanced at the bedside clock. Her lids sprang open. Ten-thirty! She'd set it for five. What the heck had happened? She jolted upright and scanned the room, searching for Jay. Had he already gone into the lab?

A sinking feeling settled low in her stomach. She needed to get hold of Erin.

She climbed from the bed. The hardwood floors felt cool beneath her bare toes. She spotted a pair of slippers near Jay's nightstand, slipped into them, and pulled on his robe.

Finger-combing her hair, she padded down the hallway. "Jay? Are you here?" She made her way into the kitchen and found a note sitting on the dinette table.

She read his familiar handwriting. He'd left the coffeepot on and fresh fruit and muffins in the fridge. Her usual breakfast.

She ran her fingertips over the words as warmth washed over her. It amazed her how observant he was, how he knew so much about her likes and dislikes.

The phone rang. She followed the sound until she found it.

"Hello." She pressed the receiver to her ear and began rifling through his cupboards in search of a coffee mug. She really needed to caffeinate before she faced this day.

"Hey, Laura. I didn't wake you, did I?" The sound of Jay's voice awakened every nerve in her body.

"No. I was just about to pour a cup of coffee."

"I'm on my way home and I wanted to see if you needed anything."

Her heart did a little pitter-patter in her chest. It was the way he said it. *Home*. It filled her with longing. She took a moment to imagine what it would be like to share a warm, welcoming home with him. To share an intimate evening after a long day at the lab. To fall into bed every night and make sweet, passionate love. She fought down the tug of emotions that swept through her.

Her throat felt tight. "I need to speak to Erin."

"I'm not at the lab. I'm in the car a block from home."

Laura nibbled on her lower lip. "Did you take the suppressant?"

He hesitated before answering. "Yes." His voice sounded strange.

"Did Erin administer it?" She held her breath.

"Yes."

Oh God!

She tried to keep her voice steady. "How, uh . . . how do you feel?" He ignored her question and asked one of his own.

"What are you wearing, Laura?" The arousal edging his voice invaded her body with panic. With excitement.

Ohmigod, Erin must have switched the vials!

Her heart rose in her throat and she felt color bloom high on her cheeks. She had to tell him her suspicions. Didn't she?

"I just pulled into my parking spot. I'm coming up." He sounded so feral, so on edge.

Laura hung up the phone and ran to the bathroom to freshen up. His scent lingered in the room from his earlier shower. The aroma stirred her senses. Pleasure shifted inside her and her whole body began to moisten with indecent thoughts.

Thoughts like what it would be like to disregard the fact that he'd been given an enhancer. To give in to her desires and make love to him. To have his naked body move over hers and to run her nails over his back while he pushed his length and thickness deep inside her.

Lost in her mind's wanderings, she didn't hear his footsteps approaching. Didn't know how long he'd been standing there watching her.

"Hey."

She spun around, met his direct gaze, and drew in a quick, sharp breath. "Hey, yourself."

She recognized that look in his eyes. It was dark, wolfish, and wild, the look of an untamed animal stalking its prey. It was the same look he'd given her just before he'd made love to her with his fingers and his mouth.

She swallowed. Hard. "Are you okay?" Her pulse began to drum and her legs went rubbery beneath her.

He edged closer, until she could feel the warmth of his body. "Not really." His voice was like a rough whisper.

She frowned in concentration. "What is it?"

He grabbed her by the waist and drew her to him. He pushed his hips into her.

Pleasure Control

She felt his erection. Her heart did a somersault. It secretly thrilled her. Keeping the pleasure from her expression, she took a small distancing step backward and plastered on an air of professionalism.

"I see." God, she wanted him so much it hurt. But it was wrong, wasn't it? To make love with him knowing what Erin had done? Knowing that he wouldn't make love to her under normal circumstances. Her botched seduction while in the tub last night proved that.

"I guess the potion didn't work after all. Perhaps we should head back to the lab and run some tests," she suggested.

Conflicting emotions passed before his eyes when she stepped away from his embrace. He grabbed her elbow and hauled her back. As her body collided with his, every nerve ending came alive.

His gaze dropped to her mouth. She shuddered as her tongue darted out to moisten her dry lips.

"Everything's working, Laura. Everything is as it should be." The roughness in his voice gave way to softness.

What did he mean by that?

"Let me make love to you, babe." The need and untamed passion in his eyes ignited her blood.

Oh God, she had to tell him. It was the right and logical thing to do. He brushed the backs of his fingers over her

189

cheek and looked at her with pure desire. Hot flames licked a path up her legs.

She opened her mouth, but no words formed. A hunger she couldn't seem to assuage moved through her when his fingers wandered lower and lower until they hovered only inches from her swollen nipples.

Suddenly she knew she was too far gone to deny herself the pleasure of his kisses, his touch. They might have no future together, but they had this moment. And for now, that would have to be enough.

What she was about to do wasn't smart—hell, it wasn't even moral—but she couldn't stop herself. After today she would never have another chance with him. She reached out and combed her fingers through his hair, guiding his mouth to hers.

Opening herself to him, heart and soul, she slipped out of his robe and let it fall to the floor. She whispered into his mouth, "Make love to me, Jay."

With her mouth poised open, Laura pressed her hot body against his and trailed her nails over his back. The cords in his muscles vibrated with each sensuous stroke.

He lowered his head and covered her mouth with his. The second his lips closed over hers, he had to remind himself how to breathe. He felt her body soften beneath his and thought he'd go crazy with desire.

Moments ago, when he'd come around that corner and had seen her standing there, looking sexy and beautiful in his robe and slippers, he felt as though he'd been sucker-punched. A fierce longing overtook him. She was an erotic combination of innocence and seduction. It was a combination that made him ache with the need to make love to her.

His erection throbbed against her stomach. His muscles trembled with need. He'd waited too long for this. There was no taming the lust in him. His control snapped as the primal beast in him took over. He needed to take her right now. Hard and fast. It was frightening how much he craved the feel of her.

Their lips separated and he inched back. As his eyes fixed on her mouth, his hands stole up her T-shirt. He nearly passed out when his fingers tangled through her damp curls.

"Christ, Laura, you're not wearing panties." She was wet. So very, very wet. He blew out a shaky breath and stroked her swollen clitoris, making it tighten in pleasure.

"They were stolen," she whispered.

He pushed a finger inside her. Her body responded and quaked at his touch. Her actions were so telling. She wanted this as much as he did. He groaned deep in his throat as hunger prowled through him.

"Oh thank God," he murmured.

Her eyes were deep, glossy. She ground her hips into his hand. "Jay, you're completely overdressed," she said, tearing at his shirt with impatient hands. "I need to touch you." Her voice was edgy, desperate.

He stepped back and tore his clothes off until he stood before her, naked and needy. She eyed his engorged cock and sucked in a breath. Licking her lips, she crooked her finger, motioning for him to come closer.

Moving swiftly, he reached under his bathroom cabinet, grabbed a condom, and quickly sheathed himself. He edged forward and closed the small gap between them. None too gently he pulled her shirt up to her waist, snaked his hands around her back until he gripped her backside, and lifted her onto his hips.

She gasped in surprise and gyrated against him. He felt her dewy folds slide open and cradle the tip of his erection.

His muscles tensed and he went suddenly light-headed as his cock absorbed the heat radiating from her sweet spot. "Wrap your legs around me," he growled.

After she obliged, he took two small steps and pressed her back against the bathroom wall.

The scent of her arousal reached his nostrils and he went mad with the need to ravish her. Within seconds, his mouth was all over hers, warm, wet, and hungry. He touched her, everywhere, yet he couldn't seem to get enough of her.

He buried his face in her neck and murmured, "Laura I can't slow down."

"I don't want you to." Her raw, frenzied voice filled him with a rush of emotions.

He swallowed and struggled to speak. "I wanted the first time we made love to be slow and passionate. You deserve that."

Her breathing grew fast and shallow. "Make love to me later, Jay. Right now I just want you to fuck me." Her shirt pooled around her hips as she tightened her legs around his back. She rocked against him until his cock breached her tight opening.

Groaning, he cupped her breasts and caressed her puckered nipples through the thin material of her shirt.

Heat raged through him. "Are you sure?" Need made his voice husky. "I wanted to pleasure you first and make sure you came." His own breathing was labored.

Color bloomed high on her cheeks. "I will come. Now, please, Jay. Fuck me." Her voice was a pleading whisper. She clenched her teeth and rocked harder. He felt the tight walls of her channel open for him.

With little finesse and much voracity, he ripped her shirt off and thrust his hips forward. He drove his cock all the way into her. She began panting as he stretched her wide open. Without giving her time to get used to the fullness, he pumped in and out of her hot, slick entrance.

She arched her back and pushed her breasts against his face. He drew one pebbled nub into his mouth and sucked until his cheeks hollowed. Paying tribute to her other breast, he covered it with his palm and pinched her dark nipple. She cried and writhed and clawed at his back.

"More . . . harder . . . please . . ." Frantic, she threw her head back and cried his name. "Jay . . ."

He drove into her so hard his balls slapped against her ass. The look in her eyes and the flush on her cheeks told him she was close.

She squeezed her lids shut.

His heart pounded in his chest. "No, baby, let me watch you come. You're so beautiful. God, I love you so much."

Her lashes fluttered open and met his gaze. Her mouth parted, but she made no sound.

A cocoon of warmth wrapped around him as he felt her sex muscles quiver. He moaned with pleasure when she reached down to stroke her own clitoris. Her hands worked feverishly between her legs. Remaining deep inside her, he rotated his hips in a circular motion, coaxing an orgasm from her. Her body tightened and a rush of liquid heat seared his cock as she came apart in his arms.

"That's my girl." Excited by her pleasure, he felt his cock begin to pulse with pent-up tension.

She buried her face in his neck. He felt her hot ragged breath on his moist naked flesh. He drove into her once again as he approached his own release. Savoring the sensations rippling through him, he impaled her again and again. Her arms coiled around his neck, pulling him closer and closer. Her full breasts crushed against his chest. With one final thrust, he felt himself let go.

He shouted and stilled his movements as he lost control of his own orgasm. She squeezed her sex around him, milking every last drop of his heated juice. His climax ripped through him with such power and intensity it left him shaking right down to his toes. He exhaled a low groan of satisfaction.

He remained inside her for a very long time. Neither one speaking, both concentrating on regulating their breathing.

Finally Laura broke the silence.

"Jay?"

"Mmmm . . ."

"My legs are numb."

He stepped back from the wall and eased her from his hips. His semi-flaccid cock slipped from her vagina. "Sorry about that." Her feet touched the floor and he noticed her wobble. He slipped his hands around her waist to steady her.

She gave him a feeble smile. "I think I need to sit down before I fall."

He gathered her in his arms and carried her naked body into the living room. Gently, he sat her on the couch. He took a seat beside her and cupped her face in his hands.

"Laura, I have a confession."

She nibbled on her lip. "I do, too."

"Okay, you go first."

Chapter *11*

God, she had to tell him. Had to tell what Erin had done. He was going to hate her for doing something so devious, for letting him believe the project failed, but she couldn't live with herself otherwise. He needed to know there was nothing wrong with the libido suppressant. She didn't want him to think his career was in jeopardy.

She laced her fingers together and stared at her lap, trying to figure out a way to soften the harsh truth. Suddenly she felt so drained, emotionally and physically. Keeping her voice low, she said, "The potion didn't fail."

His brows knitted together. "No?"

She drew a breath and blurted out, "You took the enhancer again."

She stole a peek at him, gauging his reaction, waiting for his mood to blacken. Was that amusement in his eyes? Why on earth would he be amused?

"Erin switched the vials," she said, expecting her words to wipe the grin off his face.

"She did? Why would she do that?" He put his hand on her leg. It was warm and smooth on her flesh. An involuntary shiver skipped down her spine.

She rushed on. "Because I told her I wanted to finish what we started and she suggested I switch the vials again, but I would never do that to you. I may have considered it, a time, or two, or a million, but would never go through with it. So you see, she must have done it anyway or you wouldn't have been so aroused." She was rambling, but she couldn't seem to stop herself.

His chin came up a notch. "You wanted to finish what we started?" His reaction confused her. She'd thought he'd take offense at her testimony.

Her words spilled out. "Yes. So you see, you wouldn't have slept with me if Erin hadn't switched the vials."

"Is that so?" He withdrew his hand from her leg, stretched his arms over his shoulders, and sank farther into the sofa. Her skin felt suddenly chilled at the loss of his touch. Becoming conscious of her nakedness, she folded her arms over her chest and crossed her legs.

"Why would you think that, Laura?"

"Because I'm a nerdy scientist and not a carrot stick, like your usual cuisine."

She listened as his breathing seemed to change. Tensing, she glanced sideways at him. Her gaze dropped to his exposed groin. She could have sworn his penis just twitched.

"I guess now it's my turn to confess." His voice was rough with emotion.

Hands neatly folded on her lap, she nodded. "Okay." She had no idea what he wanted to confess. She only knew it could never match the atrocity of her admission.

"Erin wasn't at the lab this morning. I called her and gave her the day off."

She stiffened, perplexed. "But you said—"

He cut her off. "I know, sorry about that."

"Then who administered the potion?"

One side of his mouth twisted up. "No one."

"What do you mean, no one?"

"I didn't take the potion."

Her head jerked back with a start. His words took the wind out of her. "What?" She nearly bounded out of her chair.

"I didn't take it," he said with an easy shrug.

Her mouth went suddenly dry. "Why not?"

He twisted sideways to face her. His eyes turned serious. "Because I happen to like nerdy science girls. One in particular."

Cathryn Fox

She gulped.

"Like you, sweet Laura, I wanted to finish what we started." His deep voice rolled over her like an intimate embrace.

Her heart flipped in her chest and she shook her head to clear it. Was she hearing him right, or was she still lost in a haze of euphoria from their unbelievable sex?

She could barely find her voice. "I don't understand."

"What's not to understand? I already told you I love you." He cradled her face between his palms and looked at her with all the love inside him. It took her breath away.

Her blood began racing. She swallowed. *He loved her.* She thought he'd only spoken those words in the heat of their frenzied coupling.

"I'm confused. Last night when I was naked in the tub I tried to seduce you and you walked out of the bathroom." Emotion thickened her voice.

A lazy smile curled his mouth. "You tried to seduce me?"

"Yeah." She threw her hands up in the air. "Okay, so I'm not so great at the seduction thing. Give me a break, it was my first attempt."

He grabbed her hand and squeezed. "Laura, I wanted to prove to you that I'm not just a sex-crazed playboy. I do think about other things." He paused for a second. "Rarely," he said, grinning. "But at times I do." He reached out and brushed her damp hair off her forehead and gazed deep into her eyes. He lowered his voice. "I could have told you I was crazy about you, but why would you believe me? You said yourself I was a playboy, that my track record wasn't so great. You're a smart girl, Laura. I figured you wouldn't believe any sweet talk coming from my mouth. I know I wouldn't have."

"You're probably right," she agreed.

"By keeping my hands off you, I wanted to prove that I care about you. All of you. Not just your gorgeous body. I wanted to show you how good we could be together outside the bedroom. You've opened my heart and shown me that I'm capable of love."

"Oh." Her voice was a soft whisper as understanding dawned on her. "I've always suspected, deep down, there was more to you, Jay. You just needed to have faith in yourself."

That seemed to please him. "And you needed to have faith in yourself, too," he added. "I love your beautiful curvy figure and your brilliant mind." He grinned and dusted a kiss over her cheek. "There is nothing sexier than a nerdy science girl," he teased. "From now on, I'm on a carrot-free diet."

She laughed as her heart began beating wildly with excitement.

He *loved* her.

He looked down sheepishly. "Of course, I'd be lying if

I said that when I saw you naked in the tub, I didn't think of sex. Wet sudsy sex." His brow rose a fraction of an inch.

She touched her tongue to her bottom lip. "Hmmm, wet sudsy sex. Never tried that." She was so completely overcome with joy, she felt giddy. A happy haze of tears began blurring her vision.

He wiped away the water pooling on her lashes. "Well, you have no idea what you're missing." His bad-boy grin returned. God, she loved that grin.

A shiver tingled all the way through her body. "Perhaps you'd better show me."

He gathered her into his arms and whisked her down the hallway. "My pleasure."

"Come to think of it, I've never had sex in the shower, or on the kitchen table, in an elevator, on an airplane . . ."

He chuckled softly. "Slow down girl, I'm only one man. We have the rest of our lives to do all those things." She saw love shining in his eyes.

She planted a warm kiss on his lips as her heart fluttered with emotion. "And you're the only man for me. I love you, Jay Cutler."

"I love you, too, Laura Cutler."

Her eyes opened wide. "Jay—"

"And you're the only woman for me. Will you marry me, Laura?" The depth of love in his voice brought on a new wave of happy tears.

"One condition." She thought her heart was going to burst as it overflowed with the love she felt for him.

He cocked his head. "Really?"

She grinned. "We never, ever try the real libido suppressant on you. I don't want to spend one single night without making love."

"Deal." He mirrored her grin, closed his mouth over hers, and carried her off to a sudsy tub to show her once again exactly how much he loved her.

Chapter *12*

Smoothing her hands over her knee-length black skirt, Laura paced nervously around the lab. She and Jay had presented their findings to the board only hours earlier and were now anxiously awaiting the results. Just knowing the members of the Grant Governing Board were three floors down in the conference room discussing their funding and future proposals made her nervous as hell.

She pulled her hair from the plastic clip anchoring it in place, shook it free until her curls spilled over her shoulder, and then glanced at Jay. Sitting on his stool, relaxed, he leafed through a magazine. He looked so handsome in his navy blue suit. The color brought out the warmth and depth in his gorgeous baby blues.

Her heart filled with love when he lifted his gaze to hers. To think a little over a week ago, they had simply been lab partners and nothing more. And now, in less than six months they were going to walk down the aisle and become life partners. Her heart leapt with joy as she relished the romantic mental image of Jay dressed in a form-fitting tuxedo standing at the altar waiting for her.

He gave her a slow, sexy grin. "Relax, Laura. They loved it." God, she couldn't believe how easily he could read her every emotion, her every expression.

She knew he was right. The board members appeared to be quite impressed with their findings, but still she couldn't help fretting. Their future careers depended on the funding.

"Do you think they'll approve our grant based solely on Bonnie and Clyde's results?"

"They'll approve our grant based on your brilliant formula, Laura," he assured her.

She smiled at his endorsement.

A knock sounded on the lab door. She glanced up to see Erin poke her head in. "The director wants to see you two right away."

"Time to go," Jay said, his blue eyes bright with excitement and anticipation. He stood, crossed the room to stand before her, and clasped her hand in his. He arched a brow. "All set?"

She blew out a breath she hadn't realized she was holding. "Let's go."

Erin wished them luck as they passed her in the hall. A few moments later they stood outside the director's office. Laura starched her spine, drew a deep fortifying breath, and knocked.

"Come in," Reginald called out.

Since they had been keeping their relationship a secret until after the results were announced, she eased her hand out of Jay's. Reginald didn't approve of office affairs and they didn't want anything interfering with their funding, their future proposals, or their ability to work together on those future projects, should they be approved.

Jay twisted the knob, pushed the door open, and motioned for her to enter.

She glanced at the director's expressionless face in an attempt to read him as she padded across his polished floor and took a seat in a plush chair across from his mahogany desk. Jay followed suit, and sat beside her in a matching chair. To stop herself from fidgeting, Laura linked her hands together and sat up straighter in her seat.

Reginald leaned back in his brown leather office chair. It creaked under his weight. His brows knitted together. "Just to keep you two up to date, Max has been arrested." Nodding his head, he gestured to a spot on the floor. Laura glanced over to find her duffel bag.

"They found your bag at Max's apartment. That and the print found at your apartment were enough to formally charge him."

Reginald lowered his voice, shook his head, and went on to explain. "Ad-Tech got wind that you two were working on a top secret project, so they planted Max here on an information-seeking mission. When we hired him, we had no idea he worked for the competition. Naturally, he neglected to mention his position at Ad-Tech on his résumé," he added, fisting his hands. "And because he had connections on the inside, his security check came back clean. After an in-house investigation, everyone who was responsible has now been removed from our organization."

Reginald's eyes softened as they focused on Laura. He folded his hands on his desk. "I apologize for that, Laura. He somehow got through the system. It won't happen again. I know I said this before, but I can't say it enough. I truly am sorry about the break-in at your apartment and I'm sorry you were caught in the cross fire."

His sincerity touched her. She offered him a warm smile. "Thank you."

He turned his attention to the manila file before him and flipped it open. "Now, I'm sure you two are more interested in the board's decision than you are in Max."

They both nodded in unison.

A broad smile stretched across his face. "That minor setback was not detrimental to your careers. Congratulations, your funding has come through. The board was impressed with your presentation, all your hard work, dedication to the project, and the positive results on Bonnie and Clyde."

Elated and a bit relieved, Laura clasped her hands together. "Yes," she said.

Jay leaned forward. "And our future proposal?" he asked eagerly.

"Funding approved," Reginald said. "You can begin preliminary trials on Pleasure Prolonged this winter." He slammed the file closed and glanced at them. "Good work, you two. Go announce it to the others."

Both grinning like the Cheshire cat, they stood. Laura grabbed her duffel bag and hurried to the door, where Jay waited for her.

"Oh, and Jay, one more thing," Reginald said.

They stopped midstride and turned. "Yes?" Jay asked, still smiling.

"Stay the hell out of my bathroom. That's not the kind of employee bonding I approve of."

Laura's smile crumbled. Ohmigod! Mortified, Laura opened her mouth to gasp, but no sound came. She felt heat and embarrassment color her skin and warm her body.

Jay cringed. "Shit," he mumbled under his breath. "Sorry about that."

Anxious to flee, Laura rotated on the ball of her foot, and gripped the doorknob like it was a lifeline.

Her escape was halted when the director said, "One more thing."

She swallowed, dreading what was coming next. Her face tightened as she turned back around.

He arched a warning brow and pinned them with a glare. His voice had taken on a hard edge. "If you two ever decide to test the drug on yourselves again, without written consent or before positive preliminary results with the lab rats, I'll kick your asses to the curb. I won't have my two best employees risking their health. Understood?"

They both nodded.

It occurred to her that Reginald truly and genuinely cared about his employees. Maybe he was on to something with all those bonding sessions.

Jay furrowed his brow. "But how . . . ?"

Reginald raised his palms in a halting motion. "It's my job to know everything." He waved a dismissive hand. "Now go, celebrate. Drink. Eat. Do what young people do. Just stay out of trouble."

They turned to leave. "Oh, and Laura?"

Her pulse leapt in her throat. Damn, she'd almost made it to the hall. Gulping, she twisted back to face him and brushed her hair from her face. What now? Was he going to comment on her pasta-making skills? Her ripped panties? She worked to find her voice and school her expression.

Her stomach tightened. "Yes?" she asked, trying to keep her voice light.

He winked at her. His eyes were playful and full of warm sincerity. His voice softened. "Congratulations on the engagement."

Laura grinned and shook her head in utter amazement. They never should have tried to get anything by Reginald Smith, a.k.a. Pit Bull.

"Thanks," she said.

"Veronica and I look forward to an invitation."

Jay reached out and caught her hand. She leaned into him and absorbed his warmth. "You can count on it," she assured Reginald. Suddenly it dawned on her. This pit bull really was just a pussycat at heart.

Reginald turned his attention back to the files in front of him. "Now go. You two have a celebration to attend," he repeated in a firm voice. "And a wedding to plan."

Laura and Jay's Christmas wedding reception had been in full swing for over an hour. Sitting next to Erin at the bar, sipping a strawberry daiquiri, her gaze skated over the guests. She took a moment's pause to consider how wonderful things had been between her and Jay since they'd fallen in love six months ago.

She smiled at her mother and father, and her new family, Isabella, Tony, and Dino, as they all sat around an intimate white-linen-covered table and engaged one another in conversation. The love in their eyes when they glanced her way warmed her all over. She nodded to Reginald and Veronica as "Reggie" shook his groove thing to some sixties song that he'd requested.

Chuckling, Laura turned her attention to Jay. Love rushed to her heart as she admired her husband from afar as he mingled so easily with their guests.

Husband. That word made her smile.

As though sensing her eyes on him, he tilted his chin until their gazes locked. He looked good enough to eat in his dark tuxedo and thigh-hugging dress pants. Of course, she had every intention of doing just that. But it would have to wait until later when she had him alone, all to herself, she mused. Straightening on her stool, she worked to stomp down her arousal for the time being.

As though reading her naughty thoughts, he gave her a sexy, knowing wink from across the dance room floor. Her heart soared with joy. The love he felt for her was obvious in his expression.

Laura couldn't have been happier. After she'd fallen into Jay's arms that warm summer night, everything else in her life had fallen into place as well. They'd secured the grant needed for further testing of Pleasure Control and their proposal to produce a serum designed to give men prolonged erections and multiple orgasms had been approved. Jay was just dying to test that one out. Not that he needed it. He'd proven that fact to her numerous times.

Since she and Jay were flying to Hawaii for an extended honeymoon in a couple of hours, they, along with the director, had decided to hand over the head scientist position for Pleasure Prolonged to Erin. This was Erin's opportunity to make her mark in the scientific world and advance her career to the next level. For the following months, she would be working closely with Kale Alexander, Jay's buddy and best man at their wedding.

Kale had agreed to take a leave of absence from his lab in Los Angeles and had come to Iowa, his old stomping grounds, to fill in for Jay while he was away.

Laura twisted sideways to speak to Erin. She looked so beautiful in her pale blue maid of honor gown, her long nutmeg colored hair, which she usually wore in a ponytail, was arranged on top of her head in a classy, artful coiffure. Her beauty was stunning.

A grin curved Laura's mouth when she noted the glazed look in Erin's eyes as she gawked slack-jawed at her handsome new lab partner, Kale. Oblivious to his admirer, Kale gracefully glided around the dance floor with a pretty young blonde. Laura noted a line of women anxiously awaiting their turn in his arms. In fact, they seemed to be tripping over their hems just to get closer to him.

Laura tapped Erin's shoulder, drawing her attention. "If you want him, seduce him, that's what I'd do," Laura whispered, throwing Erin's words back at her. "And you might want to wipe the drool from your mouth, Erin," she teased. "It's not very becoming."

Erin's mouth opened and closed in a silent gasp. "Very funny."

Laura chuckled, remembering how Erin had threatened to switch the vials on her. She never did know for certain whether she would have done it or not. Of course, it wouldn't have surprised her. Erin was one heck of a brazen girl.

Jay's powerful muscles bunched as he crossed the room and came up beside her. She shifted to face him. She pulled in a breath as a shiver skipped down her spine. Instinctively, she leaned into him. His eyes were dark and full of desire as they locked on hers. Laura's heart fluttered in her chest as she gazed at him in rapture. Her throat tightened with emotions.

He pitched his voice low. His breath was hot on her neck. "All ready to go to the airport?"

Laura noted the arousal edging his voice. His deep tone bombarded her body with feminine need. He slipped his arm around her waist, anchoring her to his muscular body. God, she loved being held by him. A thrill ran through her as his heat curled around her and fired her blood.

"I'm all ready," she said. Before she slipped away with Jay, she leaned into Erin and whispered, "Maybe you two will have as much fun testing Pleasure Prolonged as Jay and I had testing Pleasure Control."

Although she'd love to stick around and hear all the details, she had other, more pressing matters on her mind. Like how in a few short hours, she and Jay would join the infamous Mile High Club.

Besides, the details of Erin and Kale's quest to produce and test Pleasure Prolonged was an entirely new and different story . . .

Epilogue

Epilogue

A half hour into their flight to Hawaii, Jay leaned over Laura and asked in a hushed tone, "Are you wearing those panties I bought for you?"

Warm familiarity seeped into her skin and filled her with want. A wave of excitement curled around her as his mouth skimmed her cheekbone. Just knowing in a few minutes, once the overhead movie started and the cabin lights dimmed, that Jay planned on initiating her into the Mile High Club made her tremble with need. Over the past few months not only had Jay catered to her every fantasy, her every sexual whim, he had introduced her to a few she hadn't even known she had!

"You'll have to wait to find out," she teased, fluffing her pillow and adjusting her blanket over her legs.

His grin turned lethal. "The hell with that." He slipped his hand under her blanket.

"Jay, what are you doing?" she whispered, glancing around nervously. The flight attendant stood only a few seats away as she made her rounds with the drink cart.

He pitched his voice low. "You wanted to join the Mile High Club, didn't you?" He began lightly massaging her sex through her skirt.

She gave a breathy moan. "Yeah, but not here." *Oh God, that felt good.* "We're still in our seats."

He shrugged.

"Someone could come," she warned.

He grinned. "Haven't we already been through that?"

Slowly he began to draw her skirt up higher. Her breath stalled as his warm fingers drew lazy circles on her sensitive skin. A rush of heat warmed her cheeks.

Holy cripes!

Her resistance crumbled like burnt toast. She widened her legs in an encouraging gesture. Her pulse kicked into high gear. "This is very naughty, Jay."

He arched a brow. "I know."

She drew a shaky breath. "We shouldn't be doing this."

"You don't think?"

She gave a tight shake of her head and inched her legs open wider.

His fingers trailed higher over her spread legs. "Your mouth says one thing, Laura, but your body says another," he countered, his grin cocky.

Okay, so he had her on that one.

His padded thumb connected with her soft bristly hairs. His eyes darkened with desire; his throat worked as he swallowed. "Jesus," he hissed as he cupped her bare sex.

Laura chuckled as his body reacted to her nakedness. She pitched her voice low to match his. "I hope you don't mind that I'm not wearing the new panties you bought for me, but I thought it would save time." She crinkled her nose. "And the bathrooms are small, not much maneuvering room."

"Fuck, do you know what that does to me?" he growled as he dipped into her silky heat, his finger breaching her opening. The stab of pleasure between her legs made her quake.

Her vision went fuzzy. She had to work to speak. "Oh my," she said with effort.

He parted her nether lips and in one slick movement he ran his finger all the way from the front to the back. "You are so fucking hot, Laura. My cock is throbbing. I can't wait to plunge into you." His rich voice rolled over her, filling her with want and desire.

A whimper lodged in her throat as she sank farther into her seat. Excitement coiled through her as he burrowed a finger in deep. "Ohmigod," she murmured, clutching her armrests. She felt her nipples tighten, clamoring for attention.

His thumb circled her clit. She began pulsing, tightening. She shifted, providing him better access. He continued to stroke her with expertise, pushing her desires higher and higher until she thought she'd go up in a burst of flames.

Just then the flight attendant came along. "Can I get you something to drink?"

Thank God her tray was down and the woman couldn't see Jay's hand working feverishly between her legs.

Laura swallowed the dryness in her throat and tried not to sound breathless. "Water, please," she croaked out. Jay applied more pressure to her clit as his fingers stroked her with an urgent, primal hunger.

"I'll have the same," he said, his voice a little rusty.

He rolled her hard nub between his fingers, pinching and pulling until it swelled and poked out from its fleshy hood. Pain and pleasure mingled into one.

"With lots of ice," Jay added, his grin turning wickedly naughty.

The attendant's eyes narrowed in on Laura. "Are you feeling okay?" she asked.

Jay dipped a finger into her and stirred her silken heat.

Lord almighty. She was going to come. Right there. On the spot. With the flight attendant watching.

Laura nodded and gave a feeble smile. "I'm . . . okay."

"Are you airsick? You look flushed." The attendant's gaze panned her body.

Jay stroked her harder, faster. Pressure began building between her thighs, making coherent speech almost impossible.

Laura drew in a sharp breath and fanned her face, hoping to draw the woman's attention away from her blanket. "It's dry in here. I'm just a little thirsty."

The attendant's eyes focused on the blanket dangling around her feet.

Shit!

Jay piped in, "You do look a little flushed, Laura."

She stole a glance at Jay. He just sat there with an innocent look on his face as his fingers worked inside her, slowly building her orgasm.

The flight attendant put two plastic glasses of ice water on the tray in front of her. Jay grabbed one, took a huge slug, and popped an ice cube into his mouth. It clinked on his teeth and filled her with heated memories. As he swirled it around his mouth, he whisked his thumb across her clit with single-minded determination.

The attendant's eyes narrowed in concern. "Why don't you remove the blanket?"

Cathryn Fox

Soft quakes grew stronger as pressure brewed in her sex. "No, she blurted out. "I like the blanket." With slow tormenting circles that drove her mad, Jay concentrated his attention on her engorged clitoris.

The woman gave her an odd look and then reached up and turned on the cool air. "Maybe you should go to the bathroom and splash some water on your face."

"Yeah, Laura. Maybe you should go to the bathroom. You look a little feverish." Jay added another finger, filling her to the hilt. Jesus! Her heart beat in a mad cadence. Moisture broke out on her flesh. When he stirred his fingers, her body immediately responded with a hot flow of release.

The attendant backed her cart up, giving her room to enter into the aisle.

Her sex muscles began to undulate and throb. She swiped at the perspiration on her forehead. "O . . . kay," she cried out as a powerful orgasm tore through her and wracked her body. It shocked her, how intensified her climax was at that altitude.

Struggling to recapture her breath, she took a moment to right herself and then turned her attention to Jay. "You are so going to pay for that," she whispered.

Jay pulled his hand out of her damp, pulsing sex, adjusted her skirt, and straightened in his seat. His laugh was rough in anticipation. "That's what I'm counting on."

* * *

Jay scrubbed his hand over his chin. Laura's sweet feminine scent clung to his fingers. Desire fired his blood as he inhaled the intoxicating aroma. Bottled-up lust rose to the surface, demanding to be sated.

"Perhaps I should help you, Laura. Your legs seem a little wobbly." Ignoring the attendant as she gave him a curious look, Jay followed Laura to the small bathroom at the back of the plane.

As soon as the door shut behind them, Laura climbed onto the counter and opened her legs. "Jay, I'm wet and ready for you to plunge into me." Her dark eyes smoldered with need as they met his.

As much as he ached to plunge into her hard and fast until they both cried out in bliss, his mouth ached to taste her hard nipples as they pushed insistently against her blouse.

"Show me your breasts," he demanded, unable to mask the urgency and emotion in his voice.

Complying, Laura drew a quick breath and unbuttoned her top, exposing her bare breasts.

His breath hitched. His body hummed with pent-up need. A surge of heat rose in him as her gorgeous nipples darkened and tightened before his eyes. Leaning in, he circled her velvety areola with his tongue.

"Mmmm . . ."

She arched into his mouth. "Oh, that feels so . . ." Her

words died away as his thumb slipped between her open legs and brushed over her hooded flesh.

"I love how wet you get for me," he whispered over her naked, quivering flesh. His fingers circled her clit. He could feel her muscles rippling, tightening, and aching for his thickness. He closed his mouth over her nipple and drew it into his mouth, ravishing her with dark hunger.

"Please . . . Jay . . . fuck . . . me." Her fractured words urged him on. "I want more. I can't get enough," she pleaded.

He slipped a finger inside her and turned his attention to her other nipple. He brushed his tongue over her nub, wetting it, and then blew lightly until she groaned in pleasure. Her sex muscles immediately tightened and drew him in deeper. Fuck, she was so close.

"Does this fill you, Laura?"

She threw her head back and moaned. "No," she cried out, her voice full of sexual frustration. The heat in her eyes licked over him as she begged him to take her.

He wiggled his buried finger in her slick heat and slipped another inside. Applying pressure to the spot that made her moan out loud, he asked, "How about this, sweetheart? Does this fill you?"

She gyrated her hips. "No, Jay. Please. I want your cock inside me. I want it hard and fast." He could hear the impatience in her voice.

Laura slipped her hand down the front of his pants and gripped his cock. A violent shudder overtook him as she stroked and squeezed and brushed her fingers over the juices dripping from the tip. It was all he could take.

In one fluid movement, he unzipped his pants and released his pulsing dick. He pulled his undershorts down and let them hover around his knees. He gripped Laura's legs and spread them impossibly wider, exposing her pretty pink sex to him. He stood there for an extra moment, taking pleasure in the erotic view before him.

Groaning his approval, he drank in the luscious, inviting sight. "So beautiful," he said, leaning into her.

He knelt down, positioning himself between her legs and lightly brushing his tongue over her sweet sex. Her breath came in a low rush as her sex juices flowed. He lingered there, reveling in her exquisite taste, inhaling her aroused aroma. He loved how she gave herself over to him, how intimate and uninhibited they'd become.

She trembled and panted. "Oh yes," she cried out as his tongue dipped into her heated core.

Standing, he positioned his cock at her entrance as his mouth found hers. They'd given up using condoms a few months back when they decided they wanted a family. Jay was sure he'd never get used to the erotic, mind-blowing feel of skin on skin when he entered her heated body. Nothing had ever felt quite so exquisite.

He gazed deep into her passion-drenched eyes and then kissed her with all the love inside of him. "I love you, Laura."

"I love you, too," she murmured into his mouth as she bucked forward, driving his cock into her scorching heat. Fire pitched through him as her muscles sheathed his rock-hard erection.

She gripped his shoulders and cried out in heavenly bliss as he plunged into her.

Her powerful orgasm hit him by surprise. It always amazed him how responsive she was. He let out a sharp breath as her sex muscles tightened and undulated around his cock like a glove.

Gripping her hips, he angled her for a deeper thrust. He pumped into her hard and fast the way she liked it as his thumb slipped between their bodies and applied the perfect amount of pressure to her clitoris. Her sexy moan told him how much she liked it.

The depth of penetration and the feel of her creamy essence dripping over his cock sent his passion soaring. His breath came in ragged bursts.

She tipped her hips forward, forcing him in deeper. He pumped into her. In no time at all his slow strokes turned into fast, steady thrusts.

She slid her fingers through his hair. "So good . . ."

Laura murmured. Together they established a rhythm, both giving and taking at the same time.

A low growl sounded deep in his throat as pressure began building inside him. Perspiration broke out on his skin.

"Come for me, Jay," she whispered into his mouth.

His gaze moved over her face. Her dark eyes were clouded with love and desire. His heart twisted. God, she took his breath away.

Sparks shot through his body as he gave himself over to his climax. Growling, he held her tight and stilled his movements as his cock pulsed and throbbed and filled her with his seed.

Laura squeezed her sex muscles, milking him of his every last drop. She kissed his cheeks, his nose, and his mouth.

"That was amazing," he said, and cradled her in his arms for a long time as his cock grew flaccid and slipped from her sex. She snuggled in tighter. Her lashes tickled his cheeks when she blinked. A short while later Laura broke the comfortable silence.

"Jay, I was just wondering." Her voice was a low velvet murmur.

Breathless, he leaned back and stared into her glossy eyes.

"Yeah?" He brushed her hair from her forehead and pressed a light kiss to her mouth.

She gestured with a nod of her head. "Do you have something about doing me in bathrooms?"

He chuckled softly. "Sweetheart, I have something about doing you *everywhere*."

Next in the Pleasure Games series

PLEASURE PROLONGED
by Cathryn Fox

Turn the page for a sneak peek . . .

"A gorgeous hunk of a guy like that could make any woman forget her morals."

Erin Shay's gaze wandered down the length of her new lab partner, Kale Alexander as he gracefully guided Hooker Barbie around the dimly lit dance floor.

With the exception of herself, the rest of the women in the bridal party hovered in the corner around a plump Christmas tree, clucking like chicks in a hen house when the rooster strutted in. She couldn't blame them, really. With a hot bod like his, Kale was every woman's fantasy.

If she were a good girl, perhaps Santa would wrap him up and tuck him under her tree. A devious grin that would rival the Grinch's curled her painted lips.

Pinching her eyes shut, she shook her head to clear it

from its delicious meanderings. How in the heck could she be expected to work side by side with that sexy distraction for the next month without losing focus on her task?

She darn well had to find a way because her career advancement at Iowa Research Center hinged on the success of their project. It was time to stop drooling over her temporary lab partner and concentrate on their assignment.

Perched on a stool, she gestured for the bartender to bring another strawberry Daiquiri and worked at schooling her wayward thoughts. When the love ballad ended and Jingle Bell Rock boomed from a nearby speaker, her curious glance drifted back to Kale, despite a hard fought battle to look the other way.

Raven black locks that were a tad too long for office standards brushed his collar as he bent forward. Warm tingles rushed through her bloodstream as she imaged how those silky strands would feel caressing her naked flesh. Taking an extra moment to indulge in the erotic slideshow, she watched him whisper something into Barbie's ear before backing away.

She noted with mute satisfaction that Hooker Barbie, otherwise known as Deanne Sinclair, a junior research scientist from her department who had fought valiantly for Erin's new lead position, appeared to be quite miffed by his sudden departure. What a pity, Erin mused.

As Kale negotiated his way through the crowd, he shrugged off his tux jacket, tossed it over a broad shoulder, and rolled his cuffs to his elbows. With easy, casual strides

that displayed his self assurance and charisma, he saun-
tered toward the bar.

Toward her.

As she leisurely admired him from afar, visions of sugar-
plums danced in her . . .

Wait. Her brain skidded to a halt and backtracked. She
drew a breath and tried again. Visions of their assignment
to test Pleasure Prolonged, a drug enabling men to have
prolonged erections and multiple orgasms, danced in her
head.

She smiled. There, that was better. Back on track.

Hell, who was she kidding? Work was the furthest thing
from her mind. The man was a walking wet dream and her
skin grew warm every time he came near. Her smile crumbled as her gaze swept over him once again.

Good Lord, if he looked that delectable in a tailored tux
she could only imagine how scrumptious he'd look out of
it.

And imagine, she did!

Beginning with his linebacker shoulders, she visually
undressed him. Every magnificent inch of him. Proceed-
ing from the unbuttoned collar of his formfitting dress
shirt, her gaze began a slow descent. She felt her pulse race
as she traced the pattern of his wide chest, sculpted arms,
and tight waist. Her inspection halted and lingered at the
junction between his impressive muscular thighs.

His black dress pants molded to his legs like hot wax to
a candle. Her breath hitched, her pulse raced. Holy

Mother of God, he looked like he was packing a nine iron behind his zipper. The provocative mental image of where she'd like him to sink his next putt flashed through her mind like a lightning storm. A shiver tightened her stomach while a rush of liquid heat dampened her silky panties. She bit back a breathy moan as beads of perspiration dotted her forehead.

If Santa could read her mind now, the only thing under her tree would be a humongous lump of coal.

Sitting under the multicolor strobe light, her whole body vibrated and moistened with indecent images and for a brief moment she wondered if her flesh glistened like the silvery garland shimmering on the Christmas tree.

Kale's lazy gaze sifted through the crowd and settled on Erin. Ripples of sensual pleasure danced over her skin, inciting tiny goose bumps to pebble her flesh when his piercing blue eyes searched her out. Seconds seemed to crawl into minutes as she held his lingering glance. Enticing lips turned up over perfect white teeth as he flashed her his trademark bad boy grin, a grin capable of charming the skin off a snake, or the dress off a lascivious maid of honor.

Sucking in a shuddery breath, she linked her fingers together, and brushed her tongue over parched lips.

"No doubt about it. With Kale swinging the driver, one thrust would guarantee him a hole in one."

"Excuse me? What was that you just said about morals?"

Damn, she hadn't said that out loud, had she? Erin reluctantly tore her gaze from Kale and twisted around to

face the bride. God, the sight of Laura in her wedding
gown took Erin's breath away.

Clearing her throat, Erin slanted her head sideways and
tapped her nails on the bar. She furrowed her brow and
glared at her best friend in mock annoyance. "Shouldn't
you be on your honeymoon by now?"

Laura grinned and ignored the question. She smoothed
her fingers over the bodice of her dress. "By the look on
your face I'd say you'll be the next one dressed in white."
She leaned forward in her seat, her eyes wide. "Perhaps
you'd like to borrow mine."

Erin scoffed, held her hands up in a halting motion and
gave a defiant shake of her head. Tendrils of hair slipped
from their moorings and tumbled down her shoulders, coming to rest on her pretty blue, strapless maid of honor gown.

"Uh uh. Forget it. Not me. No way am I going to tie the
noose . . . I mean knot." She rolled her eyes heavenward
and cringed like she'd just eaten rancid sushi.

Laura chuckled easily and brushed Erin's hair from her
shoulders. Her voice softened. "He who protests the
most—"

With a wave of her hand, Erin cut her off and finished
the sentence. "Has the weakest argument. I know, I know.
But trust me it's not a path I ever plan on traveling. Men
are good for one thing and one thing only. Sex."

Visions of herself walking that path, or rather, church
aisle, had been squelched years ago. After coming home
early from work one day to retrieve a forgotten file, she'd

found her fiancé howling like a hound, going at it doggie style in her bed with his slut secretary. What really pissed her off was that the cheating, lying bastard had felt justified in his actions. He'd been quick to inform her that men had certain expectations and special needs and not only had she failed to live up to his, he assured her that no man in his right mind would ever put up with her long hours at the research center.

So she'd been working extra shifts at the lab to build her career. Was it a crime to want to focus on her future, to strive for success? One little bump in the road and Dwayne had taken the first exit instead of supporting her when she'd needed it the most.

Since that eye-opening incident she'd decided she didn't want or need a man in her life. As long as she had her career, she had all she needed. No man was ever going to control how she lived her life, or determine how many hours she spent at the lab pursuing her dream.

Erin pushed a wayward curl from her forehead and pressed her lips into a fine line. "I'm into simple, casual, uncomplicated sex," she said with conviction.

She sighed as the bitter truth dawned on her. Besides her ex-fiancé, Dwayne the Dog, she'd only slept with one other guy. In all honesty, she was all talk and no action. Obviously her strong physical reaction to Kale was her body's not-so-subtle reminder that it was time for a little less conversation and little more action. Good Lord, now she was quoting Elvis. She was in worse shape than she realized.

Pleasure Prolonged

"A hump and a bump, thank you, chump," Erin reinforced. She sank farther into the cushiony seat of the stool and folded her arms across her chest.

"Is that right?" a deep, sexy masculine voice sounded from behind her. "How interesting. I've never quite heard it put that way before."

Erin spun around, came face to face with Kale, and nearly bit off her tongue.

Kale leaned against the bar and let his gaze drift over Erin's soft curves and sculpted angles. He studied her flawless features and took his sweet time to appreciate the exotic beauty before him.

One word came to mind. Exquisite. Billowy nutmeg curls framed her heart-shaped face and tumbled in disarray over the bare flesh of her delicate shoulders. A sexy pink flush bloomed high on her cheeks and he fought the impulse to caress her, to see if her face was warm to the touch.

He regarded her for a quiet, thoughtful moment, wondering if that seductive blush inching its way over the silky column of her neck would travel all the way out to the peaks of her well-rounded breasts. Breasts that had been coloring his dreams, as well as his every waking thought, since sharing a dozen or so cramped car rides with her over the last week as they traveled to and from the pre-wedding activities.

"Casual, uncomplicated sex." Nodding in agreement,

Kale echoed her sentiments and raised an inquisitive brow. "Is there any other kind?"

Erin's pretty pink tongue darted out to moisten plump, cinnamon painted lips.

Cinnamon. His favorite. He'd spent countless hours fantasizing about smothering those smooth lips of hers with his own to see if they tasted as sweet as they looked. His muscles bunched and pulsed in heated anticipation as fire pitched through him. Well, at least one muscle in particular.

Locking her arms tighter over her chest she said, "Not to me." She gave a defiant tilt of her head, but for a fleeting second he detected conflicting emotions in her expressive brown eyes. Her breathing hitched and she broke eye contact with him. With her long black lashes fluttering nervously, she glanced around the room, looking everywhere but at his face.

Her bizarre reaction didn't escape him. Her nervous gestures and body language spoke volumes. Erin Shay wasn't as nonchalant about sex as she led everyone to believe.

Erin unlocked her arms and exhaled what appeared to be a relieved breath when the bartender arrived with her drink. Clearly no longer wishing to pursue their conversation, she twirled on her stool, leaned forward, and wrapped her fingers around the wide, frosty glass. With an innocent sensuality that aroused all his senses and rocketed his hormones into hyper speed, she poised the pink straw inches from her glossy mouth and parted her delectable lips.

Christ, he really wished she hadn't done that.

Kale gulped and felt his blood rush at the sight of her luscious mouth and fleshy lips. Lips designed for kissing.

Him.

Everywhere.

Now.

Fuck!

Her tongue snaked out and drew the straw inside. Puckering her mouth, she took a long suck, mirrored a sexy bedroom purr, and swallowed the icy concoction.

Desire twisted inside him as a burst of heat shot straight to his groin, making it tighten painfully. He suspected this woman had no idea how sexy she was or that she'd been getting under his skin for the past week. Hell, since the minute he'd looked into her seductive eyes, the attraction was instant, potent, all-consuming, and anything but casual. There was no denying how much he wanted her. And right now the sight of her wet, sensuous lips wrapped around that long, tubular straw filled his mind with all kinds of wild and wicked images.

Kale eased himself onto a stool and draped his tux jacket over his lap. He angled closer, close enough to breathe in her arousing, feminine scent. His nostrils flared as her hypnotic aroma curled around him and seeped under his skin. She smelled like a fragrant spring flower on a warm sunny day. Heaven help him, he'd make a deal with the devil himself to be the bumblebee in charge of pollinating that blossom.

He exhaled an agonized groan and clenched his jaw. If he didn't banish his thoughts and curb his desires, his jacket would soon be performing a magical hovering act.

When she swirled on her stool, their outer thighs connected. Lust clawed its way to the surface and clamored for attention. A thin sheen of moisture dampened his skin. The soft scrape of her silky smooth leg against his drove every sane thought from his passion-rattled brain.

Without fully considering his actions, he reached out and brushed a tendril of nutmeg hair from her delicate shoulder.

Would the silky curls at the apex of her legs be the same buttery soft texture, the same rich color?

Surprise registered on her face and she flinched at his intimate touch. Her warm hand darted out and closed over his. The sweet friction of skin rubbing skin made his cock pulse and thicken.

Twining a wavy curl around his finger, his hand hovered near the creamy swell of her full cleavage for an extra second. Long enough for him to absorb the heat radiating from her naked flesh. Gorgeous chocolate, come-hither eyes stared at him in utter shock.

She shivered under his invasive touch. "What are you doing?" Erin asked. Her tone may have sounded alarmed, but the spark igniting her eyes told an entirely different story.

Wondering what color the soft tuft of curly hair between your thighs would be if you were drenched with passion.

Pulling his hand away, he swallowed. Hard. Like he had a dry piece of steak lodged in his throat.

"Your hair was about to dip into your drink." *And I was about to come on the spot.* He thought it best to keep that last thought to himself.

"Oh." She blew her wispy bangs off her forehead. With lips close enough to taste, her sweet, strawberry scented breath wafted across his face. His mouth salivated, eager for a deeper, more thorough taste. A fever rose in him. He had no idea what kind of spell she had over him but he wanted her with a passion he'd never before experienced.

As she ran her finger around the perimeter of her glass, his thoughts fragmented. How could she make such an innocent gesture so damn erotic? He shifted to alleviate the tight ache in his groin.

"Thanks," she murmured, her voice dropping an octave. "You'd think my hair had a mind of its own." Her low chuckle sounded rough, edgy. She brushed a few loose strands from her shoulder and grinned. "So much for sitting under the dryer for hours." Rolling her eyes, she lifted one slender shoulder and gave a resigned sigh. "That's why I usually skip the salon and pull it back into a ponytail."

"Fancy hairstyles don't really fit you, do they, Erin?" He liked that about her. She was perky, earthy, natural, and beautiful without high-priced hairstyles and layers of makeup.

It occurred to him that Erin was the antithesis of the women from his social circle in Los Angeles, superficial women caring only about their needs and desires while pretending to have depth and empathy for others. After spending the last week around Erin, Kale could see right through her bad girl act. He caught glimpses of a woman who was full of warmth and compassion pretending to be superficial, something his every instinct told him she wasn't.

How interesting.

"I noticed you always wore your hair tied back during rehearsals." He gave a slow nod and paused to consider her a moment longer. "It suits you. I liked it that way."

She laughed in response and shot him a wary look. The low, throaty bewitching sound of her aphrodisiacal tone rolled over him.

One perfect eyebrow arched. "That's a first. I always thought men liked a woman's hair long and loose, so they could run their hands through it." Wiggling her fingers, she mimicked the actions.

A casual shrug curled his shoulders. Shutting out the din of the crowd, he lowered his voice and nestled closer. He pressed his body against hers and put his mouth near her ear. "Yes, well, I guess I'm not like most men."

A doubtful expression crossed her face but she didn't respond. Breaking contact, she twisted sideways, pursed her lips, and took another long suck from her straw.

Hell, those plump lips of hers looked like they were begging to be kissed.

His dick sprang higher, as though hoping to glimpse the woman who was causing all the southern commotion.

Fuck. His twenty-one gun salute had just blown his ability to stand for the next ten minutes or so. Unless he wanted everyone in the room to know he was sporting the mother of all boners, he'd have to remain seated. He closed his eyes in distress and muttered curses of sexual frustration under his breath.

Before his control completely obliterated, he redirected his thoughts and called on a cock-taming trick he'd learned back in junior high school. He thought of football, basketball, soccer, anything with balls. Damn, that wasn't working. He had balls. And right now they were in a goddamn uproar.

As his mind drifted back to the gorgeous woman beside him his dick refused to cooperate. Step aside, Houdini, and make room for the amazing Kale Alexander and his gravity defying jacket.

Jay came up beside Laura. Kale adjusted his coat, thankful for the distraction. He cleared his throat and shook his head hoping to lift the fog from his lust-filled mind.

"Time to toss the bouquet," Jay said, wrapping his hands around Laura's waist in a protective manner that had Laura's eyes brimming with the love she felt for him.

Laura planted a warm kiss on Jay's mouth and slid from her stool. Kale still found it hard to believe that "Wildman Jay Cutler" had finally settled down and gotten married. Although, in all honesty, he had to admit that he'd never seen his best friend happier.

As Kale watched the loving couple for a moment longer,

he acknowledged the pang of envy that rushed over him and sat heavy in his heart. It left a hollow, empty feeling in the pit of his stomach.

Six months previous a surprise phone call from his best friend, Jay, announcing his engagement and asking Kale to be his best man, had acted like a catalyst for Kale, causing him to take pause and consider the path of his own future and his playboy lifestyle.

Now, being back in his hometown, around his family, old friends, and familiar surroundings, made him realize how truly discontented he was with living in Los Angeles. Years ago a university scholarship had sent him west with promises of happiness and financial success. He'd only found the latter. Earning the head wing position at Castech Research Center, Iowa Research Center's parent company, had given him the financial security he'd strived for, but his playboy, bachelor lifestyle no longer brought him happiness. In fact, it left him feeling restless and unfulfilled.

Kale's gaze swept across the room, acknowledging all the familiar faces. Packing up and leaving everything behind to journey to the coast hadn't been easy for him, but he knew he had no choice. His father's death fifteen years previous had left him shouldering the responsibility of his younger sisters. Since his mother's secretarial job barely put food on the table, Kale knew the position in Los Angeles would afford him the funds needed to help take care of her household finances and put his two younger sisters through college.

Pleasure Prolonged

Although Kale enjoyed his position at Castech, he'd come to understand Los Angeles wasn't a place where he wanted to settle down for a lifetime and raise a family. And he definitely wanted a family. Now he was just waiting for the right woman to come along. One who stirred him physically, emotionally, and shared the same values and beliefs. Up until a week ago, he had begun to question whether such a woman existed.

Laura slipped her arm around Erin's shoulder. "Come on. Time for you to catch a bouquet."

"No way," Erin protested, shrugging away. She sliced one hand through the air, her voice elevating an octave. "There are plenty of single females here who'd die to catch it. I'm not one of them." She planted her feet on the rung of her stool. A spirited fire burned in her dark brown eyes as a pink tinge colored her cheeks.

When Erin spotted the determined look in Laura's eyes, she angled her chin in defiance. "Forget it, Laura—" Her words died away when Jay swiftly removed her drink from her hand.

Laura winked at Jay. "Thank you, honey."

Giving her no reprieve, Laura hauled Erin from the stool and dragged her to the dance floor. Kale grinned and watched the action with mute fascination.

Where the hell was an arena full of mud when you needed it?

"What's the matter with you?"

The sound of Jay's voice broke his concentration.

"What?" Kale twisted sideways to face his best friend and wiped the smirk from his mouth.

Furrowing his brow, Jay scrutinized Kale and signaled the bartender. "If your tongue hung any lower you'd be tripping on it. I've never seen you so distracted by a woman before." Jay accepted two cold beers and handed one to Kale.

Kale rolled his tongue back into his dry mouth, grunted something incoherent, and drained half the bitter liquor in one gulp. Much better. Now if only he could soak one other body part in the amber elixir.

Ignoring the discomfort pulling at his ever tightening groin, he took another long haul from the bottle. Fuck, he needed a cold shower. Either that or he was going to find himself in a tug of war with the palm twins when he got home. His palms. A home remedy guaranteed to relieve tension and reduce swelling.

"She's a ballbreaker, Kale," Jay warned. "Not your type at all."

Kale's bottle hit the bar with a thud. "Yeah? You think so?"

Jay scoffed. "I know so," he said with certainty. "I've seen her in action."

Kale had his suspicions. There was something about her that led him to believe otherwise. He sensed a vulnerability about her that she took great pains to guard. Gut instinct told him the bad girl act was just that. An act. A façade. One he suspected she was interested in exploring further.

Pleasure Prolonged

Damned if he, and only he, was going to be the one to help her along with that journey. And in the process he was going to get to know her on a deeper level and show her that sex between them would be anything but casual.

"You have no idea what you're getting yourself into." Jay shook his head and patted Kale on the back. "She's a maneater. She'll chew you up and spit you out, pal."

A slow grin curled Kale's mouth. "That's what I'm counting on."

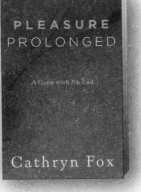